HALL-HALSELL SCHOOL

The Phantom Stallion

A PENNY OF PAINTROCK STORY

The Phantom Stallion

BY Jane and Paul Annixter

Illustrated by Robert Schultz

GOLDEN PRESS

 New York

FOR JANEY M., SANDY P.,
SUSY, AND ALL THE OTHER GIRLS
WHO WANT HORSES OF THEIR OWN

Contents

1

Midnight Must Wait

THERE WERE CLOUDS OVER PAINTROCK THAT MORNING UNTIL the breeze lifted and whisked them into tatters over the peaks. Now the high June sunlight and the cobalt sky were bringing out the colors in the rock spires that gave the ranch its name, streaks of rusty rose and pink and copper, and the rarefied air was almost warm. It was a perfect mountain day for their workout with the horses, Penny thought, with Russ Armstrong riding Janus who knew everything but Greek,

11

and she on her own beautiful Midnight who was learning so fast.

"Before you know it you'll have a five-gaited wonder horse there," Russ had said at the last lesson, "to say nothing of his being just the handsomest black in the State of Wyoming! I mean it, Penny. Our black Shiloh with all his ribbons and records hasn't a thing on Midnight. As far as that goes, they look enough alike to be sire and colt, and more and more I'm convinced that they are."

Midnight had been foaled by her father's favorite mare, Gray Alice, but his siring was a question. In the Linstrom Horse Record Book, one of the last entries Penny's father had made read: "Midnight, out of Gray Alice by Pitchdark, the wild stallion of the Wapiti Range." But there was a question mark after Pitchdark's name. The Wapiti stallion was a near legendary creature; also, as her father had known, there was a strong possibility that Midnight's sire was Shiloh, the blooded stallion belonging to the Armstrongs, the Linstroms' nearest neighbors.

Since Midnight's special training had begun, Penny felt certain that it was Shiloh. Only generations of thoroughbred saddlestock in his ancestry could account for the speed and ease with which Midnight was answering to training. Also, as Russ pointed out, Midnight had the pride and elegance as well as the intelligence and loyalty of the thoroughbred. When Penny had seen the wonderful Shiloh in his paddock it was like looking at her own horse at seven instead of two, the same handsome high-held head, long fine neck and high set tail. When Shiloh whinnied with exuberance and went sweeping round his paddock, his movement and fire were Midnight's own.

There was still another point of resemblance—her horse's bad habit of "lock-picking," which Rūss said Shiloh had had also, until they built stockades that no horse could get out of. Penny wished mightily that there were such stockades at Paintrock. As it was, there was scarcely a knot Midnight could not untie or a gate he could not unfasten when the urge was upon him to high-tail it for the hills.

Today Penny had planned on grooming her horse before lesson-time, but her Aunt Celia from Rhode Island was coming to the ranch for a visit and there were many extra things to do indoors. Her mother's only help was Mrs. Keeler, the cook, with a few hours now and again for heavy cleaning from Mrs. Engstrom, the barn man's wife. This morning, besides tidying up her own room Penny had cleaned the silver and dusted the living room furniture. It was Midnight's noonday feeding time before she got out to the corral.

He was watching for her, head high, ears pricked with eagerness and the white star-mark on his forehead agleam in the sunlight. As always, a surge of thankfulness went through Penny that he was there. "My horse!" she thought, as if she had not marveled at it hundreds of times before.

Her father had given Midnight to her when he was still a long-legged, shaky little foal. But what made a horse really yours was the love and patience that went into his care and training day after day. It was Penny herself who had put the first rope around Midnight's neck, so gently that he did not even know it and went right on playing. He learned to come to her call, not only because he was hungry and thirsty, or tired, but because he wanted to be close to her. Later, while Midnight was learning the saddle, Penny herself learned patience and responsibility in the long, slow process. First, her arm across his back, then a surcingle, then a folded blanket and finally herself! She rode him bareback for a long time before trying the saddle. So slowly and lovingly had Midnight been "broken" that it seemed never to have happened at all, but just was. From the beginning they had been fond friends, dependent on each other for their happiest hours of companionship.

Midnight neighed welcome, throwing up his head. He couldn't just stand there waiting until she got to the gate, he had to thunder around the corral at a full run, then around a second time before she could unbar the gate. His uncut mane and tail were streaming, the muscles under his silky black coat rippled and flowed.

In the corral shed that served as Midnight's stall, Penny measured his midday feed of mixed grain into the trough, and with a pitchfork loosened and shook out some six pounds of alfalfa hay. The grain was a luxury item at Paintrock Ranch, where steers being fattened for market were the only pampered animals. On summer range, cattle and horses grazed on the wild grasses and only those that were in daily use got hay. But thoroughbreds needed grain for "conditioning, appearance and performance," and Penny insisted that her horse get proper fare.

Midnight's full run became a trot, then a slow prancing walk, then a full stop beside her. Hungry as he must be, he left off munching to bunt her shoulder gently, asking for the bridle.

"I know," Penny said, "you're as anxious as I am for our lesson this afternoon! Well, be patient; it's dinnertime for me, too! I'll be back as soon as I can to give you a good brushing."

At Paintrock, dinner was at midday, and any of the Linstrom hands working close in ate with the family. Today there were only five of them in all at the long table that would seat fourteen. Penny's brother, Ken, sat in her father's old place, her mother opposite. Rudy Simms and Vic Corby were across from Penny, who was alone on her side of the table, Solly Green's place empty beside her. Solly, who was ranch foreman, had driven in to Brennerton for supplies that morning and had not yet returned. Nels, the barn man, and his wife cooked for themselves in their own quarters, the original log cabin that had been built by Grandfather Linstrom years before.

Mrs. Keeler brought in the steaming platters and tureens of food and set them down, ranch style, in the middle of the table for everyone to help himself. When her father was here, mealtime had been hearty and cheerful, with much robust talk of ranch concerns, riding, weather and high-country sports, for Carl Linstrom had loved every phase of mountain life and was in close accord with his riders. Even after more than a year Penny still missed his voice and laughter, and so, she knew, did her mother and Ken. The meals were as hearty as ever so far as food went, but the cheer was somewhat forced.

"I do hope Solly brings some word from Celia today," Laura Linstrom said. "Her last letter was vague about just when to expect her."

"I hope he brings us some news about that mystery animal playing hob out on range," Ken said. "None of the riders I've talked with seem to know any more about it than I do myself."

"They know it's a hoss," Vic Corby said. "And they know it's black."

"Has anybody actually *seen* him?" Ken asked.

"Far as I know they're all 'heard-tell' stories," Rudy Simms said. "Like Early Yates tellin' what Link Joslyn says he seen."

"Exactly," Ken said. "That's the way fables start. But a couple of those breaks in the line fence are real enough, and I'd like to know what's doing it. I asked Solly to sound out ranchers from our locality if he ran into any."

Penny's thought was that if there were a bad horse loose on range it meant added danger for Midnight those times when he got away. It always worried her when he was gone because up-country, where he most likely wandered, there were cougars and even a cattle-killing grizzly known to the upland ranchers. What fun it would be to show Midnight to Aunt Celia! Penny said now:

"I wonder if Aunt Celia still likes to ride. She used to ride old Huldah, and I'd be on Sue and—" She stopped short. "And Dad would be on Gray Alice," Penny had been about to say, but nowadays she and Ken were very careful not to mention their father's name. It was all right if Mother spoke of him first, but there was no use saddening her with reminiscences of their own. "It's been so long since Aunt Celia was here," Penny changed her tack. "Over four years—because I was only ten then! Midnight wasn't even born for two years after. Aunt Celia just won't believe it when she sees him!"

"She won't believe it when she sees *you*," her mother said. "You've grown so, Celia will have to look up at you the way I do."

It was still somewhat strange to Penny to be taller than her mother. People always said that Penny favored her father in looks. She had his blue eyes and fairness and his nice white teeth to smile with. In summer, Penny's light hair bleached in the sun "pale as prairie grass," her father used to say, and her skin turned nut brown in contrast. Lately Penny had begun to fear that she was going to have her father's large bony nose—the Linstrom nose—instead of the small straight one that made her mother's face so soft and appealing. Her mother was a true lady in all her ways and tastes, meant for a sheltered indoor existence which to Penny was only the small half of life. The best part was the freedom and constant adventure of high-country living and all the events and excitement of the ranch year.

"I do hope we can keep Celia for a while," her mother was saying. "She's free to stay, I should think, with Jeannie married and poor Horace gone. It will be so nice to have someone of my own again. We two were the closest in our family. To think—both of us widows now."

"We'll keep her all right," Ken said. "We'll just see that she stays the summer, Mom!"

In ways like this Ken was so understanding, Penny thought. He had not even glanced at Mother as he spoke, yet you could tell she felt much better now. What would Mother have done without Ken this last year or so? Penny gave the platter of braised beef a little shove toward Vic, whose plate looked sort of empty, and he helped himself. Vic had been out on range for three days checking on fences and water holes.

"Were there many new calves, Vic?" Penny asked.

"Plenty!" he said. Smile crinkles appeared round Vic's gray eyes but the rest of his weathered face was solemn. He turned to Ken: "Fences are broke down in four-five places between us and Stoddard land," he said. "Looks like some wild maniac animal tore 'em out. I mended what I could; the rest'll take new wire and more'n one hand. Them far water holes—" Vic shook his head. The upper half of his forehead which his hat covered was paler looking than usual for he had a fresh coat of wind-burn. "Never seen 'em lower this time of year. And that ain't all! The grass on most of the slopes ain't developin' seed."

"Seeds too scant, or are they dropping?" Ken asked.

"Droppin'," Vic said. "We're in for a drought this summer or I miss all calc'lations."

Ken's eyebrows twisted in irritation. Penny knew that quirky look. Only the scientific side of ranching interested Ken; old timers and their signs and omens merely annoyed him. It was as if Ken had been born in Rhode Island like mother. If he had his way he would be back at Columbia University completing the engineering course that had been interrupted when their father died. Penny was sorry for Ken for having to give up the thing he liked best, but Mother and the ranch really needed him. She needed him, too, of course, though they couldn't agree about horses. Ken's idea of a horse was the cow pony, "tireless, sure-footed, none of your blue-blooded temperament that no cowman can afford." His prejudice against Midnight was a constant rub.

"There's plenty of good grazing closer in," Ken said now. "And lots of time yet for rain."

"There's time all right," Vic said, "but I'm bettin' we don't get it. You can tell by the way the critters act, millin' round the water holes, fair founderin' themselves and standin' hock deep in the mud. 'F I was you I'd fence off them holes and water the stock just once a day."

Ken's silence said, "Well, you're not me!" as plainly as words could. Penny remembered how attentively her father used to listen when Vic voiced a hunch; he would even seek him out for advice on range and weather matters.

"We'll cross that bridge when we get there," Ken said. "Meanwhile, let's drop the Jonah angle."

Vic's face tautened into its weather lines.

"I guess the Armstrongs think it's going to be a dry summer, too," Penny said. "We're lucky to have the R. A. Creek to fall back on, Russ says. What does R. A. stand for?"

"Ranchers' Association," Ken said. "Vic, those broken fences will need attention right away," he added. "Solly is bringing more wire. You and Rudy had better tend to that."

The table was cleared and Mrs. Keeler was just bringing in the pie when Solly Green walked in. Like Vic Corby, Solly had worked years with her father and was like one of the family to Penny. He was the best of the Paintrock riders and had an enviable rodeo record.

"Telegram for you, M'am," Solly said, handing the mail to Mrs. Linstrom. "Been layin' in the P.O. box for three days —by the date on it—"

"From Celia, of course! My sister just can't believe that out here telegrams don't get to you till you get to them! Good heavens, she's arriving this afternoon! In an hour and forty minutes, to be exact. Well, children, if we're to meet her—and we must, of course—we'll have to dress and go right away."

"Not me, Mother, please!" Penny said. "Russ is coming over this afternoon to give Midnight and me another riding lesson!"

Ken snorted. "If there's anything you don't need it's riding lessons! And as for that horse of yours, he ought to be learning how to be useful on the ranch that supports him, not how to step a little higher and fancier than he does already!"

Solly was giving Penny one of his nice wind-carved grins: " 'Pears to me young Armstrong might take lessons from you, Miss Penny. Not a better rider in Washakie County than you, to my notion, and that on a high-fire black bombshell that plumb explodes if anyone else tries to sit him!"

"Thank you, Solly, but Midnight's not a bombshell, really. It's just that he has been used to me right from the first, and nobody else. But Ken, you don't understand! Russ isn't giving us ordinary riding lessons! He's teaching us the five gaits! Only someone used to training thoroughbreds could teach us those. When Midnight has learned the five gaits he will be as wonderful as any horse on the Armstrong ranch!"

"So what?" Ken said. "Why make a fancy horse still fancier? Did you find out anything about whatever it is that's breaking down our fences?" Ken asked Solly.

"Nary a thing. Saw Ed Hunnicutt at Bell's Hardware and sounded him out. All he knows is what one of his riders says the night-herd told him. And he didn't rightly see the critter, just heard him sounding off."

"Was it a regular horse sound?" Ken asked.

"Well, not too regular. Somethin' between a whinny and a whistlin' scream, the way Ed tells it."

"We have no time to lose," Laura Linstrom said rising. "Please hurry and change, Penny—something more appropriate than those jeans!"

2

Presents for Penny

PENNY DRESSED QUICKLY IN A BLUE LINEN SUIT HER AUNT
Penelope had sent her from New York and was ready even
before Ken. Knowing her mother would be some time yet,
Penny went out to see if Bud Lamar had come in. She was
not supposed to give orders or ask favors of the hands, but
with Bud she might risk it. He was the newest and youngest
of the Linstrom riders and very eager to please. If only she
could get word to Russ! It was awful to think of his riding

over at the agreed time and finding no one here. But Vic said
that Bud had not yet come in from the south line.

The least she could do was to leave a note for Russ pinned
to the corral gate. Penny raced back to the house for note
paper. Her town shoes and tight skirt hampered her. She
was so hurried and excited that her pen went wiggly as she
wrote:

Dear Russ: Please forgive me when you come over and
find only Midnight waiting for you. My aunt tele-
graphed that she will arrive today and Mother wants us
all to be at the station to meet her. I am so sorry, Russ.
Penny

Her writing ran all uphill. It might be better to tear it up,
but here she was pinning the note to the cedar post while
Midnight's soft nose coaxed and bunted her shoulder.

"There's no use looking for sugar in these silly pockets,"
she told him. "I'm sorry, 'Night. Things are turning out all
wrong for us today, aren't they? But we'll have our ride anyway, the minute I get back!"

Ken drove the station wagon at his usual impatient speed,
the dust fogging out behind them. Any other time this would
have been a pleasant outing for Penny, sitting here beside
Mother, both of them all dressed up and the day so perfect.
On the fences and along the roadside wild roses clustered.
June was wild rose month in Wyoming and now they were
at their height of pinkness and fragrance. Riding in the foothills these days, wild flowers made a garden of every slope,

pushing out of the very rocks—five-fingers, sour dock, evening star and fireweed. And back of it all were the rising peaks, lifting shelf on shelf into the sky.

"One nice thing," Laura Linstrom said, "Celia couldn't have struck sunnier, lovelier weather. Look at those white mountains!"

Aunt Celia was never sure which were mountains and which were clouds. The nearer pine-furred Wapitis were blue-black against the pale mass of the Elkhorn Range. Up in the Wapitis, one rode in deep shade along paths soft and silent with pine needles. In the old days she and her father had ridden those paths together. Now Penny dreamed of long forest rides with Russ Armstrong on their two wonder horses. Russ never made her feel like a pig-tail kid, the way most boys of eighteen seemed to do, but he was very busy with his studies and this fall he was going away to college. Denver U. was a co-ed school and of course there would be lots of older girls there. By next summer she would be lucky if Russ even remembered her existence. As far as that went, when he came over today and found her gone, he might be so annoyed he would drop the whole thing. She really couldn't blame him if he did.

"Penny, do stop moping," her mother said. "Really!"

They had come out on the paved road now and Ken had settled down to a steady seventy. Even so, they were only just in time to meet the limited from the east. Aunt Celia was standing on the station platform gazing unbelievingly about her, as if the tiny drab station, a mere dot in the midst of space and grandeur, could have nothing to do with any

destination of hers. Even as the three of them hurried toward
her the look did not change, and it dwelt upon Penny quite
without recognition. Then they were all together, warm and
happy in the way of families that are reunited, and the
strangeness in Aunt Celia's eyes had turned to wonder.

"I was looking for a little girl! What I see here is a young
woman!"

Walking to the station wagon, her eyes kept turning to
Penny with that new dazzled expression.

This was like being some lovely creature in a pageant. It
made everything seem special and rare, so that the thought
of Midnight waiting for her at home and maybe Russ there,
too, was romantic, like something in a book or a play. If only
they could hurry now!

But the luggage took time and Mother and Aunt Celia
talked fast and moved slowly. Even with Ken asking for the
second time, "Well, shall we get along?" they dawdled. Later
Mother thought of something she wanted at the store and
after that they all stopped at Ketterman's for ice cream. If
there had been any lingering hope in Penny's mind that they
might get back in time to catch Russ it was gone now. She
might as well relax and smile back at Aunt Celia, whose gaze
was still vaguely glorifying.

"Penny, dear, I brought you the silliest present: a leather
jumper! I don't suppose you dress up cowgirl fashion any
more, do you? That phase is all outgrown, I suppose!"

Mother laughed: "Outgrown! Celia, I'm afraid you are in
for a surprise. Penny's cowgirl phase, as you call it, had
barely started when you were here before."

"Now she really works at it," Ken said.

"But she seems so grown-up, so *chic* and ladylike!"

Penny felt a blush mounting from the V of her neck straight up. She guessed that Aunt Celia's stimulating approval would be gone the moment she saw her in jeans. Mother was saying:

"You must remember, Celia, both these children were born here in Wyoming where 'ranch style' is not just a fad but a way of life—"

"Where you can look farther and see less than anywhere else in America," Ken said. "You know how Webster described this country, Aunt Celia: 'A region of savages, wild beasts, shifting sands, whirlwinds, cactus and prairie dogs!'"

The two women were laughing, but Penny glared. It infuriated her when Ken talked like this.

"Of course you can look farther," she said. "And see a lot more, too!"

"Depends on what you're looking for," Ken said.

"Beautiful as this country is, it still overwhelms me," Mother said. "If Rhode Island is my size, and it is, Wyoming is seventy-eight times too big for me. Ken had his school years in New York and loves both East and West, but Penny here is Miss Wyoming, heart and soul. She practically lives in the saddle, just like Carl."

"Penny's saddle is on the wrong horse," Ken said. "Aunt Celia, can you feature a real Miss Wyoming on a grain-fed, high-stepping thoroughbred that's not worth his salt to a rancher? Miss Beverly Hills, I'd call her!"

"Ken, do stop teasing your sister," Mother said.

Penny was almost in tears: "Aunt Celia, please don't let Ken prejudice you against Midnight before you have even seen him! He's the most wonderful horse in the world, and you'll love him, I know. Oh, and a leather jumper, Auntie! I've wanted one just always. I couldn't be more thrilled!"

It was almost four o'clock when they drove up to the ranch house. Penny changed back into jeans and checked shirt and ran out to the corral. Midnight was watching for her and whinnied sharply, a rebuke for his long anxious wait.

"I know," Penny said. "It was awful for me, too."

Now she experienced a sense of shock mixed with relief, for there on the cedar post just where she had pinned it was her note to Russ. He hadn't had to ride over here for nothing and he had not had to read her silly old note! Just the same, there was a let-down feeling because Russ had forgotten about their lesson.

"Don't you want your bridle any more?" Penny asked.

Instead of lowering his head and opening his mouth for the bit as he usually did, Midnight had flung his head high and neighed again. An answering whinny came back. Penny went to the gate for a look. Over the rise of land to the south a rider was coming. He was still a quarter of a mile away but Penny recognized the smoothness of the gait. The horse appeared to be moving through the air on flexible springs. The rider, too, seemed to float, almost motionless in the saddle. If she had any doubts, there was the true four-beat sound of the rack executed with a brilliance and speed that was Janus' alone. Oh, to ride with that grace and ease!

Russ had not forgotten and the sun of this long June day was still far from setting. There were presents for Penny in her Aunt Celia's traveling bags, but none to equal this! She climbed to the top bar of the corral and waved.

3

The One-Girl Horse

PLEASED TO SEE EACH OTHER, THE TWO HORSES SNORTED AND whinnied, tossing their heads. Penny laughed: "Midnight's been waiting for Janus ever since noon!"

"I hope *you* haven't!" Russ said. "I tried my best to make it earlier, but a buyer from Denver showed up and Dad asked me to put Juno and Commodore through their paces."

What a lot of surprises there were in life! Russ, the one who was late and sorry instead of herself! Penny smiled.

"I hope it was a sale," she said.

"Matter of fact, it looks pretty good. The buyer is staying the night to make up his mind."

Midnight was really asking for the bit again, head lowered.

"He's sure ready to go," Russ said. "Guess you haven't had him out today."

"No. I've been busy too," Penny said. "My aunt arrived from the East. We had to drive in to Brennerton and meet her."

With an easy follow-through movement she swung her saddle from the top corral bar to her horse's back. Midnight stood perfectly still while she tightened the girth and mounted, but pranced with joy when Russ opened the gate. *Jigging*, Penny thought. Definitely not one of the five gaits. "*Give him something else to think about*," Russ had said, once. She turned his head firmly to the side, shifting her weight in the same direction, and as he quieted she quickly eased the reins as a reward.

"Good girl," Russ said, watching closely.

They were heading toward a nearby grassy slope they had used before. A slight downgrade acted as a natural restraint, Russ said, and helped keep a horse from breaking his gait.

"Let's see what he's got today," Russ said. "Walk him first."

Penny used to think that walking was something a horse just did, almost from the time he first stood up. But walking was one of the gaits, not just a lazy movement, and certainly not an excited jig. It should be flat-footed, with an even cadence, the rider urging yet restraining her mount.

"Fine," Russ said now. "How about the running walk?"

This, too, was a four-beat gait, but not flat-footed and much quicker. Midnight had seemed to know this gait from the very beginning—it was the way he preferred to walk. The trot came next, then the canter, which was actually a slow collected gallop. Russ' method was to stay with each gait until it seemed easy and right to both horse and rider, the rhythm of it burning in until both knew the feel of it and the pattern that it made in their nerves. This did not mean that he kept them at any one gait for longer than ten minutes at a stretch.

Today as they worked Russ said: "Penny, you have good hands! Maybe that doesn't sound like much, but it is. It means you keep an easy contact with your horse's mouth. You feel what you're doing to him, so you don't ever hurt him, and you get what you want out of him because he wants to give it."

Penny warmed to the tribute but was careful not to show her pleasure.

"As Mother said today, I was in the saddle almost before I could walk! I guess that's long enough to get good hands."

"Some riders never do get 'em," Russ said. "Now rest him awhile. We'll walk again."

"Do you think Midnight will ever master the rack?" Penny asked. "Today, coming over the hill, you and Janus looked about ten feet in the air—just floating!"

" 'The gait to take your eggs to market,' " Russ grinned. "Just a question of persistence, Penny. Remember what the old English trainer said: 'To teach a colt perfectly you've got to have a lot more time than he has.' Janus is five, remember. Lots of experience compared to a two-and-a-half year old. Janus has his growth now and his permanent teeth. But he's still learning and that's the best thing about him. Somewhere along the line a colt decides whether he's going to be something pretty special or just another horse. That comes in the fourth year, Dad says. It's all in the training, and not doing the wrong things—things that develop vices in your horse."

Vices, Penny thought. Like their old Booger who had been ruined in one week by a new hand later discovered to be a brute with horses. Ever since then Booger had been taking it out on everybody and everything, including his corral mates, if they got too close to him. Well, no one but herself could be blamed for any vices Midnight might have, though it was hard to see how she was responsible for his "lock-picking."

They pressed into an easy canter.

Russ said: "The thing is for *you* to learn how to rack, then coach 'Night yourself by slow stages. As you know, it's a four-beat gait, easy on the rider but hard on the horse, so you never stay with it for long. You could learn it quickest and best on Janus, the way you did the amble, by getting the rack feel and rhythm. If I could work with 'Night at the same time we'd have it made."

Penny said rather uneasily: "He likes you, I know, and he adores these workouts—"

"Let's change horses then," Russ said.

Penny dismounted. She watched Midnight's ears as Russ' hand went out to his bridle. They remained erect and friendly.

"It's all right, boy," Russ said, stroking his nose.

As Penny mounted Janus, Midnight snorted in plain disapproval, but he stood for Russ while she put Janus into the trot and the canter.

"Now try the amble," Russ said as she passed.

This was a gliding, four-cornered gait, similar to the rack but slower. Janus was trained to answer any sure hand and he responded perfectly.

"Good girl," Russ said.

"He's so smooth!" Penny said. "He really does float!"

"Well, I'm going to try your baby now, but I've a hunch he's not going to like it," Russ said.

Penny reined in to watch, hoping and fearing. Once Ken had tried to ride Midnight. Ken hadn't gentled him first, just grabbed the reins and vaulted into the saddle, wrangler-fashion. Midnight had stood a moment shuddering, then, to Penny's horror, sank to the ground and rolled over. Of course Ken jumped clear and would have tried again, but Penny cried and pleaded with him until he gave it up.

Now, as Russ put his hand on the pommel, Midnight blasted through black, spread nostrils and reared straight up. To Penny he looked twenty feet high and about to pitch over backward.

"Just what I thought," Russ said. "It's all right, old boy!"

"Oh, Russ, I'm so sorry!" Penny cried. "Such terrible manners! And I don't know what to do about it!"

"I wouldn't try to do anything," Russ said. "Midnight's manners are perfect where you're concerned. He's your horse. Just keep other people off him."

Russ was being wonderful about it, of course, but Penny was mortified. More than that, a feeling like a premonition was upon her, as if now that things had started to go wrong they wouldn't stop. She tried to thrust the dark feelings away, but in her memory was Ken's bitter resentment against Midnight.

"A darned snob and a rascal," he had said. "If it weren't for you, I wouldn't have that horse on the place!"

"Janus will stand," Russ said as she dismounted. "Is 'Night ever glad to get you back!"

As she took the reins, Midnight was ruckling and nodding in his most endearing way.

"Why can't you be nice like this to other people?" Penny said.

"Because he's a one-girl horse," Russ laughed. "Keep it that way!"

They were riding abreast across a stretch of meadowlike green, at their backs was the gold light of late afternoon. For a moment it was Penny's dream of riding together, all lessons learned. But that dark something was still hanging over her. Penny wondered if Russ felt it too. Glancing round she saw an intent look on his sun-dark, good-looking face. Unlike most men in this country Russ rode hatless and there were clean glints in his dark brown hair. He was different from anyone she knew, somehow deeper, more serious. His thoughtfulness was attractive. She could only hope that she did not seem too terribly juvenile to Russ.

Midnight seemed to be trying to make amends to her for his bad manners of a while ago. It had become one of those rare moments when horse and rider seem magically one creature of agility and grace. If only Russ could have experienced how wonderfully responsive Midnight could be.

"Well, what do you know?" Russ said. "Midnight's following suit. He's dropped into the amble."

So that was the airy lightness she had been feeling! Penny could not speak for fear of breaking it. They rode on for minutes more, the two horses moving in exact rhythm.

Russ said quietly: "Better break it now so 'Night will remember this as something *you* control."

"Wasn't it dreamy!" Penny said.

Russ smiled. "Sure was. We really hit a lick."

They had walked their horses up a long, gradual slope and now looked down on Paintrock—corrals, cattle pens, pastures, the big barn and out-buildings and the long rambling ranch house. Far to the left, in the broad pan of the valley, were the white-painted stockades and paddocks of the Armstrong place. Penny hoped it was as thrilling to Russ as it was to her, the two orderly ranches on the rolling green plateau, and behind them white peaks notching the sky. She was about to ask if he had a theory about the fence-breaking mystery-animal the herders were talking about. But Russ said:

"Two and a half months from now I'll be taking up life in a dorm with a roommate I don't even know!" He did not sound at all gloomy at the prospect.

Penny ventured: "I guess you'll like the city for a change. Lots of people and fun—between classes anyhow—"

"Lots of work and cramming, if I'm going to make it!" Russ said. "Law's like medicine—you just go on and on for years and years giving it all you've got and a lot more! But I like everything about it! Dad says the dullest old statute practically fascinates me, and it's true. Lots of times I'd read all night if Mom didn't come in and make a fuss."

That was the way Ken felt about engineering, Penny thought, with a real pang of sympathy for her brother.

"Dad can't understand it, but he's awfully decent about it. I'm lucky to be the youngest and least necessary one of the family. Nobody'll even miss me! Oh, Mom maybe—"

Penny almost said: "*I* will!" But stopped in time.

"Ken's like you," she said. "He wants to get away. What I wish is that I was all through school and could take over in his place. I could do it, I know, because I like ranching! I guess I feel the same about ranching as you do about law!"

Russ turned to look at her, but whether his smile meant approval or the reverse, Penny could not tell.

"Maybe it's just as well you're going to have three or four years to think that over," he said at last.

They were quiet on the way down to the ranch, and parted where they had met an hour before, at the corral gate.

4

Danger in the Air

PENNY'S ROOM WAS ON THE SOUTHEAST CORNER OF THE RANCH house, and the first thing she did on awakening every morning was to read the time of day the mountains told. In winter the Elkhorns' long shadow lay upon Paintrock until mid-morning, but you could tell what time it was by the growing intensity of gold that etched the high rims. Now, at a quarter to six on a June morning, only a faint silver light told that the sun was up beyond the peaks. It was Midnight's breakfast time. To Penny the habit of early rising was firmly established.

This morning, three days after her aunt's arrival, Penny awoke sitting up in bed with Midnight's shrill neigh in her ears. If the breeze was just right, she might have heard him from his corral, but this time it was a dream. In her dream Midnight stood on the edge of a cliff high above her, prancing and neighing. The cliff was dangerously steep, she could not reach him and she dared not call. All that she could hope to do was find some other way to bring her horse down. Penny was glad it was only a dream.

Her bedroom walls were lined with photographs of famous horses, her bookshelf held little besides books about horses, yet it was a girl's room for all that, with the two pink slipper-chairs and a frilled dressing table and the white wool rugs. The little French desk by the window was a present from her Aunt Penelope.

Penny dressed hurriedly, pulling on the new leather jumper her aunt had brought her, for the mountain morning was cool. Aunt Celia must have been inspired really, the fit was perfect and the creamy color was just right for her skin and hair. Nor had Aunt Celia's approval of her faded when she put on jeans and a checked shirt!

Down in the big log-walled kitchen Mrs. Keeler was already mixing the batter for hotcakes. With just a quick "good morning" Penny ran out through the chicken yard inside the old pole fence that Grandfather Linstrom had built, and on down to the barn. From there a corner of Midnight's corral showed and a qualm went through her. The starred head was not visible. Before she rounded the barn lot she knew that Midnight was gone.

The gate itself was intact, but the top bar was splintered. He had simply vaulted the fence. Standing there in the dust Penny let go and cried a little. The pain of her loss was so keen, and there was that bad dream to add to her misery. Somehow Midnight was in danger this time, Penny felt it in all her nerves. But she must control herself and not get into a state about it. There was breakfast to face.

On the way back to the house Penny met Nels, the barn man, always the first one up. Nels must have seen her tearful look for quick sympathy showed in his kindly eyes.

"So he's took off again, Miss Penny? Well, he's been gone before and come home by himself."

"Yes, but he's never jumped the fence before," Penny said.

Nels was shaking his head: "Now he knows he can do that he ain't likely to bother pickin' locks no more!"

This gloomy thought depressed her even more.

Penny's mother and aunt did not come down to the early breakfast which was served in the kitchen ell. Penny sat in Laura Linstrom's place opposite Ken and poured the coffee. No one at the table seemed aware of what had happened so Penny broke the news, trying to sound casual.

"Double doggone, that horse!" Solly said.

Ken's gray-blue eyes leveled, reading her through: "Don't worry too much, Sis. That horse knows which side of the fence his oats are buttered on!"

"Guess yes!" Vic said. "Wouldn't surprise me if he lep' right back over."

"I bet I know where he's headed for!" This was Bud Lamar. "Down by Crow Creek seep! I saw six-seven horses there yes'day, soakin' their feet. Want I should ride down and maybe bring him back for you, Miss Penny? I'd be mighty glad to."

Bud was always asking embarrassing questions like this, as if she had as much authority around here as anyone. Penny kept her eyes down knowing Ken would take care of the matter, as he promptly did:

"Bud, you're riding up-country with Rudy today. Have to cut out the rest of the Stoddard steers that got mixed with ours last week. Those broken fences set us back no end and I still don't understand it!"

Ken had other orders for the hands and Penny waited till he had finished before she asked:

"May I borrow Stonewall this morning?"

Her brother had to think about that. Stonewall was "ornery" like most cow ponies, but he was fast and the smartest cutting horse in the outfit.

"All right," Ken said after a moment, "but we've got to use him tomorrow."

Penny went upstairs to kiss her mother good morning and tell her where she was going. "Bud says he saw some horses down at the seep, so I'll check there first," she said. "Ken lent me Stonewall."

"Isn't Stonewall the one that rubs people off on trees?" Laura Linstrom asked.

Penny laughed: "They'll all try that trick—all but Midnight! He's the only gentleman in this outfit!"

"Well, I wouldn't call it gentlemanly to run away from his mistress, especially one who spends her whole time seeing to his comforts and well being!"

"Midnight doesn't do it to be mean," Penny said. "It's just that sometimes he's so full of energy that little old corral can't hold him. I didn't take him out yesterday, remember."

"Well, be careful, dear," her mother said. "And do be back before dinnertime."

After the smoothness of a gaited thoroughbred, a cow pony, any cow pony, was like changing from a Cadillac to a jeep. Stonewall's walk was lazy, his trot was short and choppy, and when pressed into his fast pace it was like a washboard road. In contrast to Midnight's constant consideration of his rider and his willingness to give all he had, Stonewall seemed to be saving himself every minute. Stonewall had ideas about where he wanted to go, too. Penny let him think he was having his own way going to the seep this morning. That way they would get there quicker.

Once out of the mountains' shadow the sun blazed on her shoulders and the southwest breeze puffing across the dry Washakie flats was sweet with the smell of sage and wild grass. The seep was a low point at the bend of Crow Creek where the waters spread through half an acre of moss and bunch grass on Paintrock's lower boundary line. The richest grazing land lay hereabouts, where selected steers were fattened for market and mares due to foal were pastured. A month from now these fields would be full of Herefords. Now there were small bunches only, lifting their white faces to gaze at her and bawl. Numbers of them had already sought the scant cottonwood shade. *Sign of a warm day*, Penny thought.

Already she knew that Midnight was not at the seep. If he were anywhere about he would be answering Stonewall's anticipatory whinnies as they neared Crow Creek. Three mares were there, standing hock-deep in water, and that was all.

Penny let Stonewall drink, wade, and crop a bit of tender grass before turning him up-country, but he did not want to leave the seep and acted as if the slight grade were killing him. Abruptly now Stonewall started to limp a little. This meant delay as he well knew, for Penny was bound to dismount and examine his forehoofs for possible injury. There was none.

A few minutes later Stonewall had forgotten the limp and was concentrating on drawing in his stomach so the saddle would slip. He always tried swelling up while the girth was being tightened, but Penny had been careful to thump him back to normal so that didn't work. Now he was veering very slightly to the left in a gradual circle that would lead them back to the seep. With a green rider this might have worked but Penny knew her directions and firmly held him to business.

It was a matter of convincing Stonewall all over again that you knew how to ride, then he would work for you.

Up along the line fence it was the Stoddard steers that lifted their heads to stare at her as she passed. Penny was lonesome for her own horse. How good it would have been to ride Midnight far up the Cold Spring trail this morning.

She missed seeing Russ, too. In the one lesson they had had since the day her aunt arrived, Midnight had graduated! As before, she and Russ had put the horses through the gaits and Midnight had followed Janus' compelling rhythm through the amble, on into the rack! For a few breathless moments they had sailed along together in that magic floating way. Two wonder horses indeed.

"It's just a matter of practice now," Russ had said. "You two don't need me any more. In fact, you're practically ready for Frontier Park!"

Frontier Park, the rodeo grounds at Cheyenne! Imagine riding Midnight in the Frontier Days parade! But thrilling as it was to have Midnight come through, it was sad to have the lessons end.

"See you," was all Russ had said as they parted.

Lost in her thoughts, Penny was unwary for the moment, and Stonewall took advantage of it. He had angled ever so slightly off trail and now took the bit, making for a low-branched pine. As he surged beneath, Penny had but a telling fraction of an instant to dodge. Evidently chagrined at his failure to unseat his rider, Stonewall bucked twice, stiff-legged.

"All right, now you've got it out of your system," Penny said.

Back in the mountains' long morning shadow, they were climbing toward the rocky shelf above Paintrock. Off to the left in a brush-rimmed hollow some cows and calves had spent the night and were still cozily bunched. Across the fence the Stoddard stock was on the move, filing slowly

down toward a water hole. Stonewall was attentive now, for
cattle were his business and he was ready for any signal.
Not only would he answer with something like polo pony
agility, but he would keep at it all day and all night if necessary. Until she and Midnight had gotten together, Penny, too,
had thought a good ranch horse was the best mount in the
world.

She was singing dolefully now as she rode along:

"I rode across a valley range I hadn't seen for years,
   The trail was all so spoiled and strange it nearly fetched
      the tears.
   I had to let the fences down, the fussy lanes ran wrong,
   And each new line would make me swear and hum this
      little song."

Her father used to sing this "Old Cowman's Appeal" when
they were out together. The memory of it went far back, to
the days when he used to swing her up behind his saddle
and ride about his work with her clinging to his belt.

"When my old soul hunts range and rest beyond the
      great divide,
   Just plant me in some stretch out west that's sunny,
      lonely and wide.
   Let cattle rub my tombstone round, and coyotes mourn
      their kin,
   Let horses come and paw my mound, *but don't you
      fence me in!*"

Penny's eye searched the heights ahead. Midnight had come this way other times when he was loose. Penny knew this from reports of herders who had seen him up here more than once. If he was up here now, where would he choose to spend the day? His steam would have been worked off by this time and he would be ready to rest, somewhere near water, most likely. There was another water hole farther up the mountain and Penny headed Stonewall along the faint animal trail that led to it.

High Hole was in a stand of mountain beech and all manner of creatures drank there, both wild and tame. Today while still a hundred yards distant, Stonewall ruckled nervously, and actually balked on the trail. For some reason he didn't want to go any farther along this path, water or no. It could mean a cat, Penny thought. All horses were deathly afraid of the mountain lion. At the sight of one, mares would even abandon their foals in panic-stricken flight. While this was not the hungry time of year for cougars, Penny had no wish to encounter one. Still, she had to check High Hole before turning back.

She forced Stonewall on. By now he was all atremble, and the reflex of his fear was strong upon Penny. Bears, too, were an abiding terror to horses. Could the Old Settler have come down from the high hills? Penny wondered. This was a she-grizzly known to all the ranchers of these parts, though she seldom ventured down below the nine-thousand-foot rims.

But there were neither bear nor cougar tracks in the moist earth around the Hole. Just horse tracks, among them Midnight's, perhaps; no way of telling. She tried the high whistle that had often brought him to her, but the silence of the woods was unbroken.

Though Penny could not tell why, the feel of this place was threatening, and she was as eager as Stonewall to get away from it.

5

Black Suspect

It was morning again and still midnight had not come home. Penny scarcely knew how to face the day, for Ken was firm about Stonewall being needed on the range. Of course there was always Booger and old Hulda to ride. But Booger would do his best to throw and trample her and Hulda would take half the day just to get up into the foothills. Anyway, even if she could ride Stonewall, where would she search?

Toward noon Penny saw Solly Green and two of the hands who had just come in from the south line in a huddle down by the branding corral. Something in the look of them meant trouble and she ran down to see if it concerned Midnight. Talk stopped as she came up, but Solly broke the silence.

"Boys brought in word of a stallion fight out on range last night," he said. "One of them was killed. Oh, it wasn't your horse, Miss Penny, 'twas a young coaly-bay, belongin' to the Hesketts, Charlie here says."

"Course, it could a' been your horse got the better of him, Miss Penny," Charlie File said. "True enough a rampin' black hoss was seen near dawn up by Moon Creek where the fight took place."

"Midnight's never been in a fight in his life," Penny said.

" 'Tain't too late for him to start," Vic Corby said. "He's near about growed up now."

"Could be the other hoss brung the fight to him," Charlie File said. "If he did, he sure got more'n he figgered."

The talk went on, the story building as it went. Penny's worried look went from face to face and settled upon Solly.

"Do you really think Midnight could have been in that fight, Solly?" she asked.

"I'd say a flat no, Miss Penny, except for that black horse that was seen by Wes Kincaid, one of the Heskett riders. Ain't many all-black horses in these parts, you know."

"But he's not all black," Penny said. "There's that white star mark on his forehead."

The two herders shuffled and hung their heads. Even Solly seemed uncomfortable.

"Did Wes Kincaid speak of a white mark on that horse's face?" Penny asked.

"That's just the point we was botherin' about, Miss Penny," Solly said. "Charlie here asked that, and Wes said yes, he reckoned it did."

"Well, there's one thing," Penny said. "We can tell when he comes home if he's been in any fight. There would certainly be marks on him."

At the dinner table that noon, Ken was questioning Vic about a new fence break which had been reported that morning in the south line. "You said about twenty head of Heskett's stock got through on our land. Any of our beeves over on their side?"

"Nary a head, far as I could tell. Seems our critters was far enough from the ruckus to stay quiet. But pore Wes, he had him a right busy night. 'Twasn't only the fight, he says. 'Twas the sounds that broke out before and after, and all of 'em plumb unnatural. That screamin' I was tellin' about. Could maybe have been a horse, Wes said. Must of been a horse, but something about it plumb lifted his hair and his critters all routed and took off for Texas. Even Wes' old Charlie-hoss was that scared he broke his picket rope. Wes says as how he was a good hour collectin' him and 'twas way past daylight 'fore he got his critters back in a piece—"

Ken heard Vic out with quirky brows and a skeptical look, but Penny listened with horror, somehow sensing far more than was said. For there *was* something frightening out there. Stonewall had felt it yesterday and so had she. Most of all she was frightened for Midnight, still wandering loose. If they were ready to think Midnight was the killer in that stallion fight, they might blame him for those other troubles too. To cattlemen, a broken fence and a routed herd was bad trouble.

"I don't see how anybody could think those awful noises came from Midnight!" Penny said. Her voice shook a little. "Midnight has a very nice-sounding neigh! I've never, never heard him scream and I just can't imagine it!"

Aunt Celia spoke up: "Don't anyone breathe a word to me against that beautiful horse! He's the gentlest, most intelligent animal I've ever seen!"

"The tough thing about it all," Ken said, "is that Penny's horse happened to be loose at the time."

"Never mind, dear," Laura Linstrom said. "I'm sure it will all clear up."

Ken turned with an order for Solly: the mowers would need a good going over to be ready for the alfalfa. So would the baling machine.

That afternoon Penny had an unexpected caller. Eileen Heskett rode over on her pinto, Patchy. Eileen was almost a year older than Penny and much more interested in town ways and clothes and boys than Penny thought she ever could be. Though the two girls were school friends and ranch neighbors—only the Armstrongs lived nearer Paintrock—they had few mutual interests and rarely sought each other out. Today in her jodhpurs, green silk shirt and white Stetson, Eileen looked like a dude ranch visitor. She had beautiful curls, though. Penny always admired the auburn lights in Eileen's brown hair.

Even before she got inside, Eileen was asking about Midnight: Had they found him yet? What were they going to do about him now that he was turning into such a dangerous killer? Penny was too outraged even to speak.

"Oh, I know how you must feel," Eileen went on. "He's terribly handsome and all, but a horse like that can cause no end of trouble."

"But there's no proof yet that Midnight was in that fight! He's been loose before without getting into any trouble," Penny answered hotly.

Eileen's eyes went big and surprised in the shadow of her hat. "But, Penny, Wes Kincaid *saw* your horse just before the fight! He was ramping and snorting and pounded right past Wes' night camp. He probably knew our horse was close by and was out to tangle with him. Anyway, that's what Wes said to Pop this morning. Wes said the sounds he made were enough to freeze your blood."

"There's absolutely no proof that Midnight made those awful sounds," Penny said. "And even a bay or a roan looks black on a dark night. Midnight's never been in a fight before."

"How do you know he hasn't?" Eileen said. "I mean, everybody knows how full of beans your horse is. That's the kind that picks fights. They're dangerous, too. I mean Pop said this morning he'd never hear of me riding a horse like that."

"Please, Eileen," Penny put a hand on her friend's arm. "Don't let Mother hear you say Midnight's 'dangerous.' She might worry when I'm out riding. You know—"

"Sure, Penny. I won't let on about a thing."

Penny's mother and Aunt Celia had come in to greet the visitor and Mrs. Keeler served them layer cake and fresh lemonade.

Eileen had an easy manner in company and answered Aunt Celia's polite questions with an enviable ease. She looked so pretty with her auburn curls and crisp new clothes that Penny became unpleasantly conscious of her worn jeans and her pulled-back-any-old-way hair. Eileen must be making a terrific hit with Aunt Celia, she thought, almost jealously.

Yet when Eileen had gone Aunt Celia said to Mother: "What a tiresome child that is. So pat and trite in everything she says."

Alone again Penny wandered out to Midnight's empty corral. If only he would come home without any telltale fight marks on him and prove them all wrong and stop all this talk before it got any worse. It was natural for the hands to make up yarns to spin by their night fires. Her father used to say that cowpokes got so lonesome out on range that they said everything twice when they got together again. But it was terrible when their tales made a monster out of an innocent, beautiful creature that you loved.

Solly had put a new top bar in place of the one Midnight had shattered, and now Penny leaned her forehead against it to say a little prayer. "Please bring him back safely. Please bring him back soon."

Feeling better now, she measured out a feeding of grain into the trough inside Midnight's shelter and filled his water pail and forked out his evening hay. As she worked a flight of magpies came down to pick about in the corral. There was plenty of grazing out on range, but by this time Midnight would be hungry for oats. Lonesome, too, Penny hoped.

Sven, one of the hands, was just bringing in the three Jerseys for milking. She waved to him.

"Not back yet?" Sven called out.

"Not yet!" she called back. "But he'll be home tonight!"

"Yah, so!" Sven moved on, head wagging.

Before going into the house Penny picked a bouquet of pinks and bachelor buttons from the front garden. She found a vase for them and put the small offering on Aunt Celia's dressing table, where she would be sure to notice them when she came upstairs to "dress for dinner." Abruptly Penny decided to "dress for dinner" herself tonight and wear a skirt for a change. She was giving her hair a good brushing when the call came from below: "Miss Penny! Miss Penny!"

She ran to the open window and looked down. Bud Lamar was standing below with a wide excited grin on his freckled face.

"Miss Penny, he's back! Your horse is back in his corral! The gate was still open so I reckoned you didn't know! Yes'm, I closed it!"

"Is he—does he look *all right?*"

"Well, Ma'am, he was in his shed at his oats. I didn't go in, just shut the gate as I went by."

"Thank you, Bud! Thank you!"

6

Cheyenne Calling

THERE WERE NO TELLTALE BITES OF STALLION TEETH OR ANY marks of slashing hoofs on Midnight's silky coat, only cuts and welts—fence marks?—and he was loaded with burrs and caked mud.

"You've got to keep that fellow in the barn now, Penny," Ken said.

"I don't see what good that will do," Penny said. "He can get out of the barn, he's done it before."

55

"Okay, we'll close-halter him as well."

"But Ken! He won't understand! He'll hate it!"

"Just too bad," Ken said.

"But it's not fair! Midnight couldn't have killed that other horse without getting kicked and bitten himself. You know that."

"He could if he got a lethal jaw-hold at the start," Ken said. "And that's what they claim he did. No use arguing, Penny. He'll have to be barn-stalled for a while."

"How long do you think?" Penny asked.

"At least until this talk dies down. We can't afford trouble with our neighbors. Another incident like that Heskett business might start a feud."

To a horse as used to freedom as Midnight was, the close-haltering was cruel. But the barn door itself was no problem to him, so haltering was the only way. Penny knew that Ken was not trying to take it out on her horse, he was genuinely worried. Wes Kincaid's story had grown as it spread and now Tony Degas, another of the Heskett riders, claimed to have seen a "ramping" black horse and heard weird equine screams on the night of the horse fight.

"Ghosty and plumb weird," Tony Degas said. "Sounds no human hoss should ever ought to make."

Now it was cutting time for the alfalfa. The first cutting was a bit earlier than usual this year because of the drought. There had been no rain since late May and out on the range the wild grass was sparse and drying too fast. Vic Corby's hunch had been right after all. Even Ken was calling it a drought by this time.

This morning Penny was driving the pickup along the faint wagon track toward the alfalfa flats where the mowers, rakes and baler were at work. The light truck rattled and bounced in the ruts, but the hot coffee she was carrying to the men was safe in thermos jugs. The crop they were harvesting this hot July morning was emerald color and vibrant in the strong light, the greenest thing in all the upland landscape.

Penny could see the baler now in the center of the great field, two men operating. One of the mowers was just passing it, leaving its long swath of fresh-cut green. The other was working at the far edge of the flat, its dry clatter hardly louder than the click of a beetle from the rise Penny had just topped. Two rakes were dragging the cut hay into mounds for the baler.

Rattling down-grade Penny gave a gay double toot, signal for the mid-morning coffee break they all looked forward to. Some whoops and yippees answered her and work stopped. Soon the men converged on the pickup.

"Here's our Prairie Lily herself with that life-givin' fluid," Rudy Simms said. His hat was tipped back, his narrow seamed face gray rather than ruddy from his labors and the heat. Cow pokes would kill themselves working in the saddle, but they hated farm labor or anything that had to do with machinery.

"Help yourself, Rudy," Penny said. "Doughnuts and sweet rolls, too! Come and get it everybody! Help yourselves!"

"White icin' and pineapple gooin'," Charlie File said. "Lemme at it!"

There were two extra hands for the haying, Wilson and Wright, their names were; both shy and silent. Penny helped fill their cups and paper plates.

"Solly says you two were in the money at Cheyenne last year," she said. "Are you planning to compete again this summer?"

"Yes, Ma'm," Wilson said. "Don't mind saying we took this job mainly to get us our entry money."

"What's your line?" she asked.

"Bronc ridin' and doggin'," Wilson said. "Wright here is some fancy with a rope. One-Rope Wright he was called on the program last year."

Wright hung his head and shuffled his feet but did not say a word.

Bud Lamar was standing close to the new hands, looking worshipful as he always did at men who had a rodeo reputation.

"I been savin' all year to get me a chance at Cheyenne," he said. "How many events can a fellow get into, I wonder?"

"How many can you qualify for?" Wilson grinned.

"Well, I don't rightly know," Bud said. "But I been practicin' with my twine on the calves and ridin' on old Booger and a steer or two."

"Yes, sir," Charlie File said. "I seen our boy at work. Put his rope on a gatepost t'other day, only he forgot the other end of it was still tied to the saddle-horn and off he sailed—"

They all laughed, Bud too.

"I expect you've seen our Solly Green ride in the Frontier Show," Penny changed the subject. "Not last year, though—"

Last year, in mourning, Paintrock had not been repre-
sented at Cheyenne. It was the first miss in many years, for
her father had loved having his ranch participate in the Big
Show. As a cattleman and a native son he had always taken
an active part in Frontier Days, and of course the family had
gone with him for the whole wonderful week of celebrations.
Even Mother had loved it. Only Ken had had no enthusiasm
for the rodeo. And now that Ken was managing things would
they ever be a part of Frontier Days again?

The men had had seconds and were going back to work.
Penny started home. If she hurried now she might have an
hour's ride before the noon meal when she would be needed
in the kitchen. The hands ate first at the big table and Penny
helped serve with her mother and Mrs. Keeler. Even Aunt
Celia cooked and helped. These days, with Midnight being
kept under such restraint, it was necessary to ride him several
extra hours. Out in the hills together they were both perfectly happy. And there were the new gaits to practice till
they were letter-perfect. If only Russ could see how smoothly
Midnight went through his paces without slip or break. Too
bad, in a way, that he was such a brilliant horse. Otherwise
Russ and Janus might still be riding with them, Penny
thought. Those wonderful days with the four of them riding
together! Would they ever come again?

Now Midnight heard her coming and welcomed her with
impatient thuds and nickers. How endless the time must
have seemed to him, standing here ever since yesterday.

"I know how you hate it," Penny said while Midnight
munched the carrot she had brought. "It hurts your pride,

doesn't it? You're no Booger, are you? All you want is to be back in the corral where you belong."

Midnight opened his mouth for the bit, actually thrusting his head into the held bridle. Then he moved to the rack that held his saddle and stood waiting. What he needed was two or three hours of brisk exercise, but she had promised to help with the dinner.

On the grassy slope where they used to meet Russ and Janus, Midnight shot, jet-powered, into a dead run. Penny gave him his head for a space, then used the "aids," as Russ called them, to slow him to a canter. ("The aids are the rider's weight, voice, reins and legs. They are the language in which the horseman communicates with his mount.") Now Midnight was whinnying and looking round.

"They're not coming," Penny said, "and it's all your fault! You're just too smart, fellow, you learn too fast!"

How heavenly it would be if they could go to Cheyenne this month, Penny thought. Why shouldn't they go? Solly was anxious to "get into the money" again. Bud Lamar was wild to go and Aunt Celia really ought to see Frontier Days. Penny was sure Mother would make the trip if Ken could be persuaded to go. Ken was the one to work on. She guessed she'd start on him this very day.

Time to turn back. Midnight could scarcely believe it. Cantering homeward across the long meadow he was as nearly rebellious as he ever became.

"Never mind, we'll go out again later," she promised him.

But Midnight was tossing his head, actually snorting with disgust at going home so soon. His mood filled Penny with qualms. Whatever happened he must not get loose right now. The mere sight of Midnight loose on range would start the night herders running for their lives. As she left him, Penny said: "Please be patient! Please be good—and maybe we'll get to ride in Frontier Park!"

7

Broken Halter

THE ALFALFA WAS ALMOST IN. SOON NOW, PENNY WOULD BE free for the hours of riding that she and Midnight needed to master their new stunt. It was not just a trick. It was better than that, for only the most trustworthy and collected saddle horse in the world could perform it.

Midnight was churning to get out of that barn and back in his own corral. She could feel him thinking about it day and night, and it worried her.

"He's not used to being treated like a wild animal or an old buggy horse," she told Ken.

"A little discipline won't hurt him," Ken said. "And if there's another incident out on range that horse needs an airtight alibi."

Evidently Ken allowed for the possibility that Midnight was blameless so far, something he would never have admitted straight out.

"Ken, do you know there will be *four* Paintrock entries if we go to Cheyenne this year? Solly and Bud Lamar, and Wilson and Wright, the extra hands. They told me they were going to sign up as Paintrock riders, too. Then if I ride in the Parade it makes five! Pretty good showing for Paintrock, wouldn't it be?"

"Good enough," Ken said. "But as I keep telling you, there just isn't time for that show stuff any more. Mother wouldn't care to go, I'm sure. Too many memories."

"Mother didn't say that when I talked to her!" Penny said. "And Aunt Celia really *wants* to go! She never has, you know; it was the wrong time of year when she was here last time. Will you *think* about going, Ken?" she pleaded.

Ken grinned at her: "Can't help thinking about it, can I— with you bringing it up all the time."

She would keep right on bringing it up then, Penny thought. Solly had promised to put in a word for Cheyenne whenever he could, and so had Aunt Celia. Riding in the Frontier Parade was her privilege as Carl Linstrom's daughter. Pride in her horse and visions of herself in cowgirl costume had Penny full of dreams.

But Midnight ran out of patience. One morning, when Penny went out to give him his breakfast, his stall was empty. The chewed and broken end of his halter rope told the story. The barn door had been easy enough for him, Penny knew; he had simply nosed up the crossbar and shoved. No telling just when it had happened, but it was sometime during the night.

"That's all we needed!" Ken said. "Penny, you'd better take Stonewall and check along the creek and down at the seep. I'll send Vic to search up-country. If any of the Hesketts saw you on Stonewall they'd know Midnight was loose and that would be enough to start talk again."

Ken seemed to be really trying to help and Penny was grateful. That morning she rode the whole five mile length of Cottonwood Creek, but there was no sign of her horse. At dinner Vic had no better luck to report.

In the afternoon Penny rode out again and searched the winding coulees branching out from Stony Creek, farther down country. She had to find her horse before dark, that was all she knew. The stories that night herders told made all the trouble.

It was Midnight himself who ended the strain. When Penny got home in the late afternoon, there he was in his own corral with the gate still open. There were no new scratches on him and scarcely any mud on his hocks. He stood to be greeted and ruckled reassuringly in answer to her questions.

"You couldn't stand it any longer in that stall, could you?" Penny said. "You just wanted to show us, didn't you? Now you're back—and you're going to stay here, aren't you?"

Later, while Penny measured out his hay and oats, Midnight trotted round and round the corral and walked pridefully in and out of his shelter.

"Just a little old homebody, if I ever saw one."

This was Solly who had paused at the gate to watch. "Plumb domestic, he is, looking into his cupboards and countin' over his stuff."

Penny laughed delightedly. "Solly, he came in all by himself and waited till I got home—I don't know how long. Surely Ken will let him stay in his own corral now, don't you think?"

"Might as well," Solly said, "seein' as how he gets his own way anyhow."

Something in his tone made Penny turn quickly: "Has anything happened, Solly?"

"Wish I could say no, Miss Penny. But I saw Jeff Stoddard a bit ago and he said Roxy Clay told him the Phantom Black was loose again last night! Roxy heard him soundin' off mortal close, Jeff said. Enough to scare his mare into a dead run with him aboard."

"Oh, Solly!" Penny wailed. "How awful for all that to start again!"

"For sure, and all our close-haltering for nothing."

Penny moved over to the gate and Midnight left his supper to follow her. "Did Roxy Clay really see the black horse?" she asked.

"Well now, all I know is what they tell me," Solly said. "Jeff asked Roxy that same question and Roxy said yes, he saw a big black somethin' come out of the dark. But he didn't linger none to watch. Truth to tell, when his mare begun to slow down he dug in his heels and whooped her on home, Roxy said."

"That just sounds silly to me," Penny said. "I think they made it all up!"

Solly shrugged. "Could be, Miss Penny, but it's a real shame this little old wander-boy of yours was havin' his night out at the time."

Midnight was bunting her shoulder for attention and Penny stroked his velvety nose. "Why doesn't anyone think of blaming Pitchdark, the Wapiti stallion?" she asked now. "Remember all the stories there used to be about him? Fights, too, and fence-breaking, just the same sort of things that are happening now."

"I remember well," Solly said. "Many's the lost mare been charged to that ol' black's account. 'The night-horse of the hills,' folks called him, and 'the wild Wapiti.' Now they got it 'The Screaming Terror' and 'The Screamer,' and 'The Mystery Black.'"

"Maybe Pitchdark *is* on the rampage again!" Penny said eagerly.

A kind of pitying look had come into Solly's eyes. "'Fraid not, Miss Penny. There's just one thing: *wild stallions don't wear shoes.* All the tracks up where that Heskett horse was killed and the fences were broke and all, was of shod animals. Vic and I rode up there special and looked the ground over and there wasn't a barefoot track in the lot!"

The finality of this shook Penny. Without realizing it she must have been holding to the idea of the Wapiti stallion as a kind of final argument in case of need. That was out now. Naturally enough, wild horses had only the bare hoofs they were born with. Besides that, as Penny well knew, there had been no reports about the wild stallion for a long time. He might even be dead.

Solly changed the subject: "How you doing with that brother of yours about Cheyenne?"

"I think he's weakening," Penny said.

"We're all bettin' on you, Miss Penny."

"Solly, I have to ask you this one question: Do *you* think Midnight is—is the one?"

Solly seemed reluctant to answer. He got out his Durham sack and rolled one of his tight, crooked cigarettes.

"It ain't that I figure he is, Miss Penny," he said at last, "but I have to go along with Ken in wishing that one of these happenin's would happen while your horse is sure enough at home."

8

Official Visitor

IT WAS UP TO PENNY TO EXERCISE MIDNIGHT ENOUGH EVERY day to keep him contented. The new stunt was coming along better than she had dared to hope and the five gaits were "burned in," as Russ had said, the rhythm and pattern of them established in their very nerves. Midnight was also learning how to stand in posed position, completely still. This was one of the accomplishments of the thoroughly trained horse. Russ had showed her how to proceed, though they had not gotten to practice it together. As with all the other exacting disciplines of his "education," Midnight took to posing naturally and beautifully, arching his neck and holding his tail high in "the proud and perfect manner." Midnight loved to learn, and the more training she gave him, the better he liked it.

Penny now had a new argument for Ken about going to Cheyenne: for the whole week that they would be away Midnight would have *the* perfect alibi! And what with no rain all this time and the scarcity of grass and water making for touchy tempers in men and animals, something else might very well happen out on range. If it happened while they were away, they might come home from Frontier Days to find Midnight cleared of all blame!

Still Ken did not commit himself, but Penny could see that this was her most convincing argument so far.

Today she and Midnight were ambling in along the lane after a full afternoon of work together. Behind them a motor car turned into Paintrock from the Brennerton road, and Penny drew over to the side to let it pass. Still in the mood of their afternoon's work, she touched Midnight with her toe on the tendon of the right foreleg just above the fetlock, and with one hand pressed his withers. He responded instantly and as the car came up they held the pose. The driver stopped and leaned out, smiling at her rather uncertainly.

"Penny? Penny Linstrom?"

"Why, Judge Kirkland! Hello!" She dismounted to greet her father's old friend.

The Judge was an ever welcome visitor at Paintrock, but it was more than a year since they had seen him.

"Mother will be so glad to see you!"

"Then it is Penny! Upon my soul!"

Penny was getting used to such exclamations from old friends not lately seen. The thrilling thing about Judge Kirkland's surprise and admiration was that it plainly included Midnight. Considering who this smiling, bespectacled gentleman was, Cheyenne suddenly seemed very close.

Though a judge of the Superior Court, it was in a capacity other than law that the Linstroms knew Judge Kirkland. For years now he had been a familiar figure in the Judges' stand during Rodeo Week at Cheyenne, and he took an official interest in all Frontier Days matters. An expert horseman and horse fancier himself, the little show Penny and Midnight had just put on without realizing they had an audience, had been fully appreciated.

"How wonderful of you to come!" Penny was saying. "But why have you stayed away from us so long?"

"My dear," the Judge said, "I did not realize it had been so long until I saw you! Obviously the little girl I knew has had time to grow up! And that handsome, admirably trained black you are riding! Don't tell me he's that colt of Gray Alice's you were gentling some time back?"

"Of course he is! Midnight is two and a half now. We've been working together a lot lately."

"So I see! That dress-parade demonstration as I drove up —the amble, in fact, perfectly executed as far as I could see! And that flawless pose! Look at him now with bridle down, the perfectly collected horse if ever I saw one! Penny, you have been busy indeed! What else can you do? Jump fences, I suppose? Turn on a dime? Vault to the saddle like a Cossack?"

Penny laughed. "We don't know too many tricks, Judge Kirkland, but Midnight has all the five gaits and now we're practicing something else rather special."

"That I shall have to see!" the Judge said.

"Of course, whenever you say!"

"What's the matter with right now?"

"But you must be tired from your long drive. And you'll want to see Mother and Aunt Celia! Do you remember my Aunt Celia from Rhode Island?"

"Indeed I do!" the Judge said. "But right now while you have him so well in hand, do show me this new 'something special.'"

Penny was breathless at the thought. "I don't know whether we're ready to show you *that* yet! But I'd love to put him through his paces for you and we'll—we'll try—"

"Good," Judge Kirkland said.

At least it was a perfect place for their tryout, the long unpaved drive, clear and straight all the way to the Brennerton road. And they were both keyed up from the long afternoon of practice.

"Well, here we go!" Penny laughed.

The walk, the trot, the canter, the amble, the rack.

For the last, the rack, Penny had turned about and was riding back toward the Judge. She waited for the perfect moment when Midnight was at the height of his stride.

Then Penny dropped the reins over her horse's neck, sat very straight in the saddle and *folded her arms.*

Without a break in the supple, almost jarless speed of the rack, Midnight swept past the car and the spellbound man standing beside it. A moment later, glowing in the knowledge that it had been a perfect performance, Penny picked up the reins and walked her horse back to Judge Kirkland.

9

The Big Parade

EVERYTHING WOULD BE FINE AS SOON AS THE PARADE GOT MOV-
ing down Frontier Avenue toward the Rodeo Grounds, Penny
thought. As it was, it was taking all she had of control and
tender persuasion to keep Midnight from jigging sidewise
right into the watching crowd. He was being a gentleman,
though, about the other horses in their group. Which was
more than could be said for the moon-eyed pinto just ahead
of them. Twice Penny had seen that one lay back his ears

and bare his yellow teeth at Madie Jensen's palomino standing beside him. The dark-haired girl on the pinto seemed
very nervous. Perhaps it was her first parade, too.

Up ahead in the grandstand, waiting to see them as they
entered the Arena, were Mother and Aunt Celia. Ken would
be watching, too, from the Judges' stand where he had been
invited to sit as a tribute to Carl Linstrom. Ken pretended
indifference, but Penny knew that he was highly pleased by
the honor and she was glad for him.

Poor Ken! He had been literally railroaded into coming
to Cheyenne, all his objections overridden by Judge Kirkland.

"Why, you *have* to go!" the Judge had said that night at
supper. "You owe it to Carl! You owe it to Paintrock Ranch!
Most of all, if I may say so, you owe it to Penny here! That
girl has accomplished something like a miracle with that
black colt of hers! Why, I saw something this afternoon that
the King of Saddle Horses himself, the great Rex McDonald,
was famed for—namely the *reinless rack!* One of the prettiest
and rarest sights in horsemanship, and Penny pulled it on
me as if it were just another gait! I want to see that beautiful
performance repeated in the Arena at Cheyenne—if I can
prevail on you, Laura . . ."

Penny still glowed at the memory of that supper table
scene. Judge Kirkland, acknowledged horse authority and
esteemed friend, literally singing Midnight's praises to the
whole table. After the dark suspicions and accusations turned
upon her horse in recent weeks, the Judge's more than
kind words had restored Penny's faith, and his comparing

Midnight to the great Rex McDonald was a tribute beyond dreams.

For years, Rex had been one of Penny's horse heroes whose history and winnings she knew by heart. Rex McDonald was among saddle horses what the immortal Dan Patch had been among harness racers, standing alone, a prince of his kind.

The Judge had extolled Midnight's intelligence, his collectedness and grace, mark of the true thoroughbred. The more he talked, the more Aunt Celia had beamed with pride, and Mother, too, in her modest way. Even Ken looked pleased. And the Judge ended by inviting the family to stay the week of the Rodeo at his Cheyenne home.

It was fortunate that he had invited them, for accommodations at hotels or tourist camps in Cheyenne were out of the question. Forty thousand people and more, twice the population of the town itself, had poured in from all parts of the country to see the Big Show. Even the tenement district and many private homes were crowded with lodgers, the families themselves sleeping in their basements or on porches to give space to the visitors. As usual, the tribe of Sioux Indians had come in from the Dakota reservation and were encamped in Frontier Park. And of course there were hundreds of stockmen and horse wranglers come to try their luck in the Rodeo.

Solly and Bud Lamar, as well as Wilson and Wright, had found lodging at a ranch just outside of town. The Judge's kind invitation had included Midnight, who had a fine box stall in the Kirkland barn.

Now a stir went through the long column and the jaded, waiting faces of the spectators began to liven up. Midnight blasted his impatience and reared spectacularly to the delight of the younger set along the curb whose whoops set the pinto into a stiff-legged dance. The dark girl in his saddle nervously sawed at the reins. The man on the albino at Penny's left muttered:

"Looks like that fellow's a troublemaker!" This was John Henderson, who would perform with his horse in the afternoon show. The albino, with his milk-white mane and tail and pink skin, was the perfect foil for Midnight's blue-black coat.

At last the whistle sounded up ahead and the procession actually moved. Penny was apprehensive about the moment when the band just ahead of them would strike up, but it came without mishap. Midnight merely pranced enthusiastically. Penny kept turning him until she had him perfectly in hand. She could not miss the admiring stares that fixed on her and her horse as they passed. Midnight was at his best again, walking in perfect cadence, neck beautifully arched as if he were proud of the ribbons in his mane and foretop, the distinguishing mark of the five-gaited horse.

Up ahead there were whoops and shouts of laughter. The first block of the pageant was made up of ancient vehicles of the pioneer days: ox carts, Indian travoix, prairie schooners, dog carts and finally high-wheeled bicycles and old flivvers that balked every now and then and had to be pushed by their goggled and bedustered drivers. It was the better part of a century's progress in transportation that was passing by and the crowd loved it.

None of the buckaroos who would go yipping and fanning their broomtails across the Arena later in the day were in Penny's group of riders this morning. These were the "fancy horses," picked for their beauty, style and breeding: palominos, Appaloosas, albinos, ruddy bays and chestnuts the color of October leaves. Some of the riders, like Mr. Henderson and Madie Jensen, were performers with acts in the show. Others were town officials or citizens showing off their fine mounts and fancy trappings. Madie Jensen on the palomino was a well-known trick rider whom Penny had watched with breathless admiration two seasons before. It was a thrill to be riding so near Madie in the big Parade. And there was a chance she and Midnight would actually appear in the Arena this afternoon!

As late as this morning, however, Laura Linstrom had been unwilling to let Penny do "that Rex McDonald stunt Judge Kirkland thought so highly of."

"We have to call a halt somewhere!" she had said rather vaguely.

"But Mother," Penny had argued. "Midnight's *trustworthy!* That's all the stunt proves, really! You know he does all the gaits as naturally as he trots! It would be *such fun* to show him off in the Arena!"

"That's all very well, Penny, but the Judge would not have been so impressed if there wasn't some *risk* about it, of that I'm certain! What if something startled your horse while you were 'riding reinless'? You'd be thrown!"

"Why should I be thrown? We've done it dozens of times and Midnight loves it as much as I do!"

"Penny, it's one thing to do stunts in some quiet meadow at home and quite another in the noise and excitement of this mad place! You're going to ride him in the Parade, aren't you? Isn't that enough of 'showing him off' for one day?"

"It's not like riding him in the Arena!"

Maybe when Mother saw how wonderful Midnight looked beside Mr. Henderson's albino and Madie Jensen's palomino she would reconsider. The last word from Judge Kirkland was that he could arrange for her to ride any afternoon with just an hour's notice.

Up ahead there were some sudden sharp sounds like gunshots and a shout. Midnight reared briefly but quieted again. The girl on the pinto seemed in real trouble. Snorting and champing the bit, that moon-eyed little beast had gone into a blind stiff-legged pitching which his rider was powerless to curb. She was staying with him, but he was much too near the close-packed crowd at the curb. Directly in the pinto's path were a mother and two small children. Penny saw them press backward in alarm, but the crowd behind them was like a solid wall.

Penny's action now was involuntary. It was just that someone had to do something and she made the first move, lancing Midnight forward into the breach, and literally shouldering the smaller pinto aside. In the moment of grace thus afforded, the mother and her children were drawn back into the crowd and the pinto girl gained control of her horse.

It was all over in an instant. Penny and Midnight were back in place, the procession moving on as before. But there were calls from the crowd:

"Good girl! Some rider!"

"Say, she rates a medal for that!"

The warm smiles that were turned her way gave Penny a heavenly floaty feeling. Mr. Henderson was smiling, too, and the pinto girl said something about "never being able to thank her."

But it was Madie Jensen who made the incident unforgettable. That glamorous personality of rodeo-land actually wheeled her mount and danced him for a moment as close as possible to Penny's horse, saying in a lovely, loud voice: "That was quick thinking, girlie! You've put all the rest of us to shame!"

10

Rodeo!

AFTER THE PARADE, MADIE SOUGHT HER OUT AND THEY TALKED about horses, a subject fascinating to them both. When Penny mentioned that there was a stunt she would like to do with Midnight in the Arena, Madie went to bat for her with her mother.

"I don't know whether you know it, Mrs. Linstrom, but your girl here is a star performer on that horse," Madie said. "She can do anything with him. Your girl's quick action this morning and her horse's perfect response saved us all from what might have been real tragedy! I've been riding in the shows for six years now, but I wouldn't be sure of getting my horse to act with anything like that speed! What I mean is, Mrs. Linstrom, any trick that kid has to show, the stands sure need to see it!"

With this, and what Judge Kirkland and others had to say —for the incident at the curb was being widely discussed— Laura Linstrom's consent was given. And so, right after Madie's own ride this afternoon, Penny and Midnight were to have their turn in the Arena.

Now she was sitting between her mother and Aunt Celia to the right of the Judges' stand, watching for Solly Green to come out of the chutes on Pallbearer, "the meanest hoss on our buckin' string," as the announcer said.

It was the second time that afternoon that the loudspeakers had announced a contestant from Paintrock Ranch. Wilson had already had his ride on Gangrene, another of the bad ones, yipping and fanning and scratching till the whistle sounded, and only once showing daylight between the saddle and the seat of his jeans. Solly would have to better that ride to be "in the money" this afternoon—and it wouldn't be an easy task.

There was a wave of noise from the stands as Pallbearer came crow-hopping across the Arena, back arched, legs rigid, four feet bunched together. Solly had style; he was a great showman. That wonderful grin, Penny thought proudly, it just never came off! The tougher Pallbearer got, the more quietly amused Solly looked.

Behind them a man said: "What can a poor hoss do, anyways, with them long legs wrapped round him and tied underneath?"

"What do you think of it, Aunt Celia?" Penny asked.

"Perfectly horrible, of course, but I love it! I wouldn't have missed it for anything!"

At last the whistle sounded and Solly slid easily sidewise into the arms of the pickup man. Pallbearer plunged on, still kicking at the sky. The crowd roared.

"No daylight," Penny said. "Not even once. A perfect score for our Solly!"

"No daylight, did you say?" Aunt Celia said. "All I can say is I'd hate to see any more. Why, I'm going practically blind in this glare."

"Celia, you make me feel like an expert!" Penny's mother laughed. "*Daylight* means that the rider has bounced in the saddle, doesn't it, Penny?"

"As little as five or six inches," Penny said.

Other rides followed, but Solly had the "day money" cinched.

The two clowns and their mule were back now, still trying to "get aboard" their animal, using a ladder this time which the mule kicked from under them and finally sat down on.

"That animal thinks he's an elephant," Aunt Celia said.

Meanwhile a creaking and splintering sounded from the chutes. The steer-riding contest came next, the announcer said. The rodeo hands were being kept busy tightening ropes and surcingles.

"Isn't Bud Lamar going to be in this event?" Laura Linstrom asked.

"Yes," Penny said, "and I don't think he has any idea what he's in for! Steer riding's just the worst!"

Penny had seen Bud across the street at noon and he was still limping from yesterday's ride on Barbwire in the bucking contest. Bud had made a fair showing in that, until the last five seconds when Barbwire "sunfished," and Bud had "sailed high and took up a homestead," as the announcer had put it. It was a hard fall with a dust-biting slide at the end. Bud must have blacked out for a few seconds, because he lay still and the ambulance came clanging in. Then, just as the stretcher men reached for him, Bud sprang up, staring around to see who was hurt. He didn't seem to know what the crowd was yelping about either, but grinned good naturedly as he limped out of the Arena.

"Dead game or a pure fool, that feller," Penny heard someone say.

"Both!" another man had answered.

She remembered something Solly had said: "Bud wants too much, too fast, and that could stop him dead before he's rightly started—unless he's fool *enough!*" Solly had added thoughtfully.

Penny wondered what "fool enough" would be. Maybe like the nice kindly fools in the fairy tales that even ogres had to help.

"Bud has paid entry money on four different contests!" Penny said now. "Calf roping and bulldogging, besides bronc and steer riding!"

"Good grief!" Aunt Celia said. "Do you mean to tell me these boys have to *pay* to go in there and get themselves half killed?"

"That's the rule," Penny said. "It's the only way they can get in. Bud said he saved up for his entries all year."

"Well, it's not fair!" Aunt Celia said.

A boy from Texas, Hobe Hall, erupted from the chutes on a black Brahma bull. He was bounced high, rolled in the dust, and sent packing. Ace Wheatly from Montana came next and made a good ride. Penny kept seeing Bud's brave grin as he limped away from the ambulance yesterday afternoon. All hump and sloping back, steers were, and bull-mean if they got a man down.

"Now watch Chute Four, Ladies and Gents!" the announcer was calling. "In just one-half minute you'll see Bud Lamar of Paintrock Ranch, the young buckaroo with the yaller shirt you saw sailing against the sky yesterday afternoon, coming out of Chute Four on Curdle, one of the toughest bovines in captivity! Peel your eye now, folks, here he comes!"

"See?" Penny said, showing her crossed fingers. Her mother and aunt followed suit.

Curdle looked the meanest of the lot, a dark brindle with a rolling whitish eye. He was the biggest, too, or looked so, with little Bud on his huge humped shoulders. He gave a bellow and went into a series of ton-heavy, ground-spurning plunges, his hindquarters lashing from side to side. *Jar, shake! Jar, shake!* "Like riding a pile driver in an earthquake," as Solly had once said.

Bud kept his left-hand hold on the surcingle strap, legs wide, his whole body bouncing and flapping. The brindle was driving straight for the stockade wall. Penny knew that maneuver: he was bent on disabling his rider by crushing his leg and hip. Somehow, at the instant of impact, Bud's leg went high. When the steer pivoted and came pounding back, zigging and zagging, Bud was still with him.

There were howls and roars from the crowd. Having missed on one side, the steer was out to rub his man off on the other side of the stockade. People were standing now. Penny had lost sight of Bud, but heard the smash just below as the heavy barrier was struck. That had been it, of course. Down at the foot of the wall which she could not see, Bud would be lying in the dust, leg mangled, hip broken, likely to be a cripple for the rest of his life.

Yet when Curdle shot out into sight again Bud was still in place, still waving his hat and taking it. The twisting and plunging went on as though it would never stop. Round about were mutters:

"That's kid's out! He's punchdrunk!" "He's froze to that strap and can't let go!"

Bud's head wobbled, a broken-neck look that must mean he was unconscious. Now it had happened; he was down. The steer ramped on for a short way, then wheeled and came back, head low, one horn dipping. The stands had gone silent.

Penny and her aunt were holding each other in a tense grip.

"We'd better not look," Penny whispered.

But her eyes wouldn't stay closed. Bud lay there apparently lifeless with the steer coming in.

Suddenly it was all right. Somehow the two clowns had got between the steer and the boy on the ground, both of them waving red cloths. The steer jinked furiously toward one of the clowns who ran and dodged, leading him away, while the other clown watched for his chance to run in and intercept.

"Angels in disguise!" breathed Aunt Celia. "I shall revere clowns from this day on."

Now the pickup men had come in. Bud sat up groggily, reaching for his hat.

"Well, folks, this is quite a day for Paintrock Ranch!" the loudspeaker said. "The ride you just saw pretty well cinches day-money for this contest, too. For a minute there it sort of looked as if we'd have to send that money to Bud Lamar's next of kin! But our boy's going to live it up himself! He's all right, ladies and gents! He's climbing up under his own power! Let's have a big hand for a really nervy rider!"

Bud needed some help, but not too much, to swing up behind the pickup's saddle.

Forty minutes later Penny, on Midnight, was waiting with Mr. Henderson on his albino and Madie Jensen on her palomino and another girl on a spotted Appaloosa, at the main entrance to the Arena. Their big moment had almost come, but how quiet and tame her performance would seem after the drama and hazard of rides like Bud's and Solly's! But in between, the stands had had an Indian dance to cool down on and a leisurely, dignified Squaw Race to key them back to plain horses. Perhaps the crowd would welcome a letdown from the tension of the steers and buckers. A gusty, refreshing little breeze had come up in the last half hour.

Madie Jensen caught Penny's eye and smiled: "That horse of yours is a born showman," she said. "As for his rider, I've got to say this: COOL. Who'd ever think there was any *first time* about this for either of you?"

Madie was so nice! It helped to know that she did not look nervous. But she was! It was not only the tameness of what she had to offer compared to the other Paintrock rides of the day, it was the established quality and reputation of her immediate group of riders: Madie at the very top of her field, known from coast to coast; Mr. Henderson, a trick rider only slightly less famous! Even the girl on the Appaloosa could make her horse waltz, bow and kneel! What was she doing in this company? What did she have to show an audience sated and jaded with almost incredible feats of skill and daring?

At least she was to be the first of the "fancy horse" group to go on, and Midnight was in high spirits and right on his mettle, and it showed. Every eye was upon him with that glow of appreciation which said plainer than words: "What a beautiful horse!" Pride in him rose in her and with it her confidence. This was Paintrock's day, Paintrock would have a perfect score.

Now her name was coming over the loudspeakers. Still another representative of Paintrock Ranch, the announcer said, and the youngest rider in the Show. With the blood of pure excitement pounding in her ears Penny scarcely heard what he said. The gate swung open and here they were alone in the Arena, the focus of some thirty thousand pairs of eyes. It was just after they had passed the Judges' stand that it happened. Someone in the first rows had let go of a newspaper and a lift of breeze caught up a sheet of it and brought it fluttering like a big white bird straight at them. With a startled snort Midnight reared and took off at a dead run.

This was the sort of mishap that could occur at any time and was no one's fault, least of all Midnight's, but how unlucky that it should have happened now! Penny's thought was that Midnight would be easier to handle if she gave him his head for the moment, but to the stands it must have looked as if she had lost control entirely. The crowd gave a great collective gasp and then seemed to hold its breath. The pickup men were coming toward her across the Arena, one of the rodeo clowns running beside them. The other clown had gathered up the blown paper and was watching from the side lines.

Penny gave the approaching men a reassuring smile and shook her head. As she had often done in the past, she leaned forward, speaking quietly into Midnight's ear. In a few moments she had brought him down to a brisk canter, to a trot, and then to a walk.

To Penny's astonishment the crowd applauded. She did not deserve this, but it was very heartwarming. Willy-nilly, Midnight had gone backwards through three of the gaits. Now they went forward through all five, circling the Arena twice in the process. When the moment came, with Midnight the fully collected horse that he really was, Penny gave them the "reinless rack." To the crowd, which but a few moments before had thought she had a runaway on her hands, the dropped reins and her serenely folded arms must have been a confounding sight. There was utter silence until she lifted the reins once more, then applause—long and sustained.

11

Taste of Glory

"YES, SIR, I HAD ME A GOOD ALL-ROUND COW-POKE IN THAT BUD-
boy before Frontier Days," Solly said.

It was Sunday dinner at Paintrock. The apple pie was on
the table and the coffee cups were full. Time to tell it again
with variations. Penny, for one, couldn't hear it often
enough.

"Used to be I could set him to line ridin', roundin' up
strays, or maybe a bit of fence mendin' now and again." Solly

looked round the table with his glinty slit of a smile. "He'd even take his turn at the baler, or run the mower for a spell, and I'd know the job would get done. But now!"

Penny smiled reassuringly at Bud sitting across from her. This ribbing came with his fame and Bud just had to take it.

"Now!" Solly heaved a big sad sigh. "Nothin' but walleyes and glory dreams whilst he runs his coin-silver hondo up an' down his shockin' pink neckerchief! Why ride herd when all a feller has to do is set on a tough steer and get his daylights knocked loose for a fat purse, and hear the crowd howl in the bargain?"

Bud was beet color, but enjoying it all just the same.

"He'll recover," Ken said.

"Well, I dunno if I can rightly live with him till then! Keeps sayin' he prob'ly made a big mistake not followin' the Show south and east. And that boy all banged up the way he was! I told him today, I said, 'Bud, luck like you had couldn't holt a day longer than it did! You'd of wound up in the meat cart before long.' Don't know as he even heard me."

"You're just bragging, Solly, and you know it!" Aunt Celia said. "Well, all in all it was the worst strain I was ever put through. And that's what you call good entertainment! It goes without saying that I practically had heart failure when Penny's horse ran away with her! But the way she handled that situation, then went ahead to show what that—that Black Beauty, that Pegasus can really do, well, it was the high point of the whole show!"

Trust Aunt Celia to see that she was properly appreciated, Penny thought, glowing in spite of herself. The whole tableful had gone silent for an instant, as much a tribute as the laughter and kidding that Bud had drawn.

" 'Twas a sight to give class to the whole proceedin's—once our princess here got her horse in hand," Solly said. "Like the king of *good* horses, he was, comin' on to restore our faith after all them bad ones."

"That was very nicely said, Solly," Laura Linstrom said. "I must say that there were a few moments there that I never care to go through again, but it ended very well."

Ken grinned. "It's a good thing Penny couldn't hear the complimentary remarks passed round in the judges' stand where I was, or there'd be no living with her either!"

"Boy! When you get a horse you can trust like that," Bud said in a tone of awe. "Give over and fold your arms on him, I mean, and him hittin' a fast and fancy clip, well, it's—"

They all waited for him to finish, but apparently no words came.

"What Bud means is you got a real rider, that's what he means!"

"No, Vic," Penny said. "It means you've got a great horse! No amount of riding or training can bring *that* out of a horse unless it's *there*."

"Boy!" Bud said again, so fervently that everybody laughed.

How strange it was that the little accident of the blown newspaper, instead of being a bad break, had really made the day for them. It had focused the crowd's attention so that the trust implied by the reinless rack seemed truly dramatic. And Midnight's charm had told, for the applause was so complete. Not the howling, stamping kind that the steer riders and bronc busters brought down, but warm and very special, a pure taste of glory. And somehow it had not seemed strange at all, just wonderfully natural and right.

What *had* seemed strange was their homecoming. For six whole days she had scarcely thought of "the Mystery Black," "the Night Horse," "The Screamer." At Cheyenne, Midnight had been admired and accepted for the gentle, high-born creature he was, cared for and trusted as a matter of course, and almost heroized after the curb incident. There had been a piece in the paper about that and people came to the Kirkland place to look at him and take photographs, till the Judge's stable man had remarked: "What that ribbon-hoss needs is a social secretary." To Penny this homage was no more than Midnight deserved. In the glow of it she had forgotten that dark distrust had ever touched him.

But back at Paintrock they found things exactly as they had left them. Vic summed it up for them in these words: "No, sir, we ain't had nothin' but peace around here since you-all left! Nary a Night Horse or a Mystery Screamer between here and the Tetons, far as I know."

"It *would* have to turn out that way," Ken had groaned. "We're right back where we were."

The taste of glory! Sweet and short! Now when Penny rode out on Midnight the looks that came their way were barbed with suspicion.

"How'd he act while you was away?" she was asked. "Kill any more horses? Sure been quiet around here this last week!"

When she tried to tell them the truth, people just laughed. So she stopped trying.

This first Sunday after their return, Penny was saddling Midnight for an afternoon ride when she turned to see Russ Armstrong on Janus just topping the rise. He came up smiling.

"Just wanted to congratulate you two on your Frontier Days triumphs!"

The two horses were whinnying with pleasure at the sight of each other and now had their heads together over the corral bars.

"How great he's looking," Russ said. "What a horse!"

For Penny the almost oppressively warm afternoon had suddenly become as rare and delectable as those first June days. "Were you coming in?" she asked.

"I was," Russ said, "but suppose we take a little ride instead."

They turned down toward Cottonwood Creek, walking the horses. Penny was giving Russ a brief résumé of the Cheyenne days, but she sensed a new kind of reserve in him, and stopped. Was he thinking about the horrid "mystery horse" stories that had been going round? Suddenly Penny had to know where Russ stood on the matter.

"It would be nice if Midnight had some of the love and trust here at home that he got from simply everybody at Cheyenne!" she said. "We hoped there would be something new on the 'Phantom Screamer' while we were away, so people would stop blaming Midnight! But nothing happened all last week! It makes it sort of suspicious looking because Midnight has been out loose every time there's been trouble!"

"It's rough all right," Russ said. "That playing hooky gets

a horse into plenty of trouble. Of course, there'd be two black suspects if it weren't for our high stockades. Shiloh'd be loose half the time if he had his way—"

"Then you don't believe Midnight has been doing these awful things?" Penny asked.

"Certainly not! In the thoroughbred saddler, gentleness is bred right into the bone. Generations of it—and blood tells! But that's something your typical western rancher would never take into account. No, Penny, it's just an unlucky break that Midnight is being blamed. There's got to be another black horse in the equation! Too bad that Pitchdark seems to have dropped out of existence the last few years."

"I thought about him, too," Penny said. "But Solly Green says they examined the ground carefully after that horse-fight and there were no unshod tracks anywhere."

"That fixes that," Russ said.

They rode in silence for a space. Relieved as she was that Russ still believed in Midnight, Penny could not help seeing that his queer reserve was still there. Maybe Russ had been studying too hard. He did look a bit pale and hollow-eyed. It was becoming though, Penny thought. It gave him an even more distinguished look. Russ was going to be a very important man some day.

They were on the woods trail in the flutter of the cotton-woods. The trees were at their summer greenest now, the leaves glinting like coins as they showed their silvery undersides in the light breeze.

"How do you like show business?" Russ asked abruptly. "Intend to follow it up?"

Penny was too taken back to answer.

"I didn't see your act," Russ said, "but my brother Jack was in Cheyenne last week and took in the show. He said you put it over like an old-timer, ending up the five gaits with the reinless rack, neat as you please!" Russ grinned at her. "Can't recall teaching you that one!"

"Well, you taught me how to teach my horse!" Penny said. "And once when you were showing me how to pose him you said, 'just take it sort of leisurely and don't push him ever. Introduce the idea, whatever it is, then go back to it now and again till he catches on. That way he can learn *any*thing!' That's what I did, Russ. I got the reinless rack out of a book," she added. "It was Rex McDonald's old stunt, you know."

"Yes, and it takes plenty of doing! You sure must have worked at it these last weeks!"

"Not as hard as you'd think, though. Midnight never gets tired and bored with trying, the way you'd think a horse would. He just wants more!"

"He's brilliant all right," Russ said, and lapsed into silence again.

Was the air clear now? Penny wondered. She found herself wishing that some of the Frontier Days glamor had stuck a bit better so that Russ could see it on her. But it had all blown away in the live prairie wind and she was just her plain self again.

"Is anything bothering you, Russ?" she asked finally.

He smiled round at her. "There was. When Jack told me about your Arena performance and the way the crowd went for it, I thought, 'Penny'll be different now, you watch!' I guess I sort of sold myself on the idea. But I was wrong, Penny, you're just the same. They didn't succeed in spoiling you and that's really something!"

Russ was talking easily again and his smile was back. As they rode on it seemed to Penny that what she had now was a real and more lasting taste of glory.

12

Mishap

SHE WOULD WEAR HER WHIPCORDS, PENNY DECIDED, A COMPRO-
mise between jeans and jodhpurs, and a fresh white blouse.
But no Stetson! Her hair could just fly! Of course it was very
nice of Eileen Heskett to suggest a ride together. It might
be fun, too, if Eileen would agree to open country. Mostly,
it seemed, her preferred bridle path was the Brennerton Road.

Two days ago, the Heskett station wagon had stopped in
the lane and Eileen, dressed in pink from picture hat to

pumps, had rushed in to propose today's outing. She couldn't stay a minute, because she was just on her way to Grace Leeper's bridal shower, but what about a ride Thursday afternoon? "Penny, we don't get together nearly often enough! I said to Mama, 'there's Penny Linstrom, one of my best friends and I hardly ever see her!' You know, when two gals like to ride the way we do! So, swell! I'll ride over this way about two Thursday! 'Bye!"

Penny was pleasantly flustered. "I didn't know Eileen Heskett liked me so much!" she said to her mother.

"Why shouldn't she, I'd like to know?" Laura Linstrom said.

Aunt Celia remarked: "That girl's the kind you can measure your general popularity by. Right now your stock must be pretty high, my dear."

"After all, the two girls go to school together," Penny's mother said, "and they both like to ride. I don't know why they don't get together oftener!"

Penny hadn't worn her whipcords for almost a year and they were a trifle tight, but pausing at her door Aunt Celia said she looked fine enough for any bridle path. "And at the same time not *over*doing it," she added, as if that were the final compliment.

Aunt Celia had come into the room and was standing by Penny's window. "I wonder what *he* wants. Well, really!"

"Who, Auntie?"

"That Bud-boy, down there looking up at your window like some love-sick troubadour!"

Penny ran over. Bud stood below, hat in hand, his round

face visibly pale under his freckles. His look was so woebe-
gone that Penny parted the curtains and called down to him.

"What's the matter, Bud? What's happened?"

"Boy! Have I gone and done it! I sure didn't mean to! I
only wanted to help—"

"What, Bud, what?"

"Well, I thought it'd be real nice if I could saddle your
horse and have him all ready for you when you came out—"

Penny had gone rigid with knowing. Such a feeling of
hopelessness came over her, as if events were moving toward
some dark, inevitable climax that nothing could forestall.

"He got away from you? He's gone?"

"I don't even know what startled him," Bud said. "He just
rared up and took off over the corral bars—"

She had been giving Midnight plenty of exercise every
day and he had seemed quite content in his roomy corral,
but it had happened just the same. Bud stood waiting for a
rebuke but all Penny said was: "Did it happen just now?"

He looked at the dust and shuffled: "Well, not just this
minute, Miss Penny. Took me a spell to work up my nerve
to tell you. Go ahead and bawl me out, I got it comin'."

"Which way did he go, Bud?"

"Straight up country."

Aunt Celia murmured: "What an unfortunate moment for
this to happen!"

Bud was still standing there. "Vic took Stonewall out, but
Benjy's here. Want I should collect him for you?"

Penny thought about it. "Yes, Bud. Please."

It was already two o'clock. Penny went downstairs to wait.

She took a straight chair by the front door, and sat very still, trying to collect herself. She did not even realize that her mother had come into the room.

"Why don't you answer me? Penny, what *is* the matter?"

If only she could hide somewhere until whatever was going to happen had happened. She did not want sympathy.

"Penny, I *demand* to know what has happened!" her mother cried.

"Midnight's gone again. Over the corral bars."

Laura Linstrom dropped into a chair. "Is that all! From the look of you I thought it was something terrible!" She added, "I'm sure it's a great disappointment, dear, just when you had planned to ride with Eileen."

Disappointment! If that were all.

Penny waited till she saw Eileen on Patchy, coming up the lane, then walked slowly out to meet her. Eileen did not see her coming. Her gaze was fixed on Bud, who had old Benjy at the hitching rack.

"Aren't you Bud Lamar, the boy that rode the steer in the Cheyenne rodeo?" Penny heard Eileen asking. "I know you must be because the one I heard about was the youngest steer rider in the contest, and you fit the description!"

"Yes, ma'am," Bud said.

"I'm Eileen Heskett. Our ranch is just a mile south of here along the Brennerton Road—if you're ever over our way! Oh, hello, Penny! . . . You were in the bulldogging contest, too, weren't you?"

"Yes, ma'am," Bud said again.

"It takes real daring to ride steers, I know!" Eileen went

on, smiling her prettiest into Bud's hot-looking, embarrassed face. "Well, I guess I'm talking to a future champion all right. Double-check, you're shy! Real champs always are, I've noticed, but nice—once you get to know them—"

"I saddled Benjy for you, Miss Penny," Bud broke in. "Just leave him in the round corral when you get back, I'll tend to him for you—" And Bud walked off, without so much as a "thank you" to Eileen.

"He's cute, isn't he?" Eileen said. "What did he mean he saddled *Benjy* for you? Where's your horse? Aren't you ready for our ride?"

"I'm going to ride Benjy, Eileen," Penny said. "Midnight— Midnight's gone again!"

"Gone where? Oh, Penny, how awful! You mean that horse is on the loose again? What happened?"

"Nothing. Bud tried to saddle him for me and he vaulted the fence the same way he did before—"

"Bud again!" Eileen said with an overwise smile. "I guess you and that boy get along pretty well—being in the rodeo together and all—"

"Our Solly Green made a record ride, too," Penny said. "And two more Paintrock men scored at Cheyenne!" She meant to put pride and enthusiasm into her tone, but her voice was somehow dull and low, the way her heart felt.

"Well, hurrah for you!" Eileen said. "Pop wouldn't *dream* of letting *me* ride in a rodeo! He says he'd as leave have me prance around in a musical show!"

The inference was unpleasant, but Penny chose to overlook it. "We can still have our ride, Eileen, if you don't mind heading up-country with me for a way. I've got to have a look for Midnight before he has a chance to get too far away."

Eileen's eyes had gone big and scared: "You don't mean you're going up into those mountains alone to search for *that* horse!"

"Why, of course," Penny said. "If we find him I can just shift the saddle to Midnight and Benjy will come home by himself—"

The horror in Eileen's big brown eyes looked real. "Count me out! With that horse loose on the range I wouldn't go up in those mountains *for anything*—not even with two strong men to guard me! The stories I've heard about that horse! Penny, you're just crazy if you go up there alone! Why, I'm even afraid to ride home alone! I wonder if that Bud Lamar would mind riding over with me?"

Penny had mounted Benjy. "I'm sure he'd be happy to, Eileen. I'd ask him for you, but I ought to be on my way if I'm to catch up with Midnight this afternoon."

13

The Contagion of Fear

FOR A MILE OR TWO, PENNY JUST RODE, SCARCELY LIFTING HER
gaze from Benjy's gray ears and spotted neck. Benjy was
bony and slow. The up-trail was hard for him. Nothing to do
but give over to his grudging, springless pace.

The uselessness of another long search was upon Penny.
She would not find him anyway, she knew. The only time
she had ever found him was back in November of last year,
in a snow storm, and then she had just happened to meet

Midnight coming down trail. He had had enough of being hungry and cold and was coming home. This time, too, he would return in his own good time; when he had tired of a wild grass diet, most likely. But what might not have happened in the meantime!

Eileen's horrified stare was before Penny's eyes: *"With that horse loose—"* Eileen wasn't putting it on, either. She was really scared, and that sort of fear was catching. Penny could feel it trying to get at her now, something like the chill that comes with fever, not caused by honest cold, just part of the sickness. What was there to be afraid of? But that was just it, you didn't need any *thing*, you just were afraid. And what Eileen would be telling people, spreading the fear, made the prospect twice as black.

If only Eileen hadn't had to be there today! If only Bud hadn't tried to be so helpful! Two things meant to be nice, and both had turned out wrong.

Penny came in sight of the main water hole, which had lately been fenced, as Vic had suggested back in June. The cattle were collecting for their late afternoon drink. It took two or three herders just to attend to the daily watering of the stock. Farther along was the shine of new wire where the line fence had been repaired. Somewhere through here was the spot where Roxy Clay had been scared by a "big black somethin'." In spite of herself, Penny felt the creep of it.

The first big pines were beginning now. Sometimes pine trees growing close enough together to touch arms seemed to know too much, and to be talking about it in wind-whispers. Years ago, riding behind her father's saddle, Penny used to think how scarey it would be without him. That little-girl feeling was upon her now, lonesomeness and creepiness and something else that she was trying very hard not to admit to herself. But it was there, and it was the heart of the whole matter.

Benjy was almost hurrying now, for they had turned into the trail that led to High Hole. On a warm afternoon like this Midnight might well go there first of all. As they came nearer, Penny watched Benjy for the signs of nervousness or alarm Stonewall had showed that other time. But Benjy was just humping along. This time it was she who felt nervous and afraid. It was not fear of encountering any wild creature, for any horse, even old Benjy bent on a long cool drink of water, would know and warn if a predator was anywhere about. The fear that was creeping over her now was worse than that. She faced it now: *It was the fear that Midnight would be there and that she would find him changed!* Not her horse any more, but some fearsome new creature, a beast that frightened men and stock and killed its own kind.

To admit such a fear was like treachery, condemning one who loved and trusted you. It made Penny feel terrible, but the fear was there just the same, poisoning her mind.

Without realizing it, Penny had been holding Benjy in. Deliberately now she gave him his head to water. It was dark near the spring as if the hours of afternoon had sped frighteningly into the mountain, racing to lose themselves in its shadow. Some clouds, the first dark-looking ones she had seen in weeks, were edging over the peaks above. Rain would be good if it came.

While Benjy drank, Penny's eyes searched fearfully among the surrounding trees. She could not bring herself to call. All she asked now was to get home again, without proving what she feared.

Penny lay in her room with the blinds drawn.

"You are not running a temperature, so it's not a virus," her mother said. "Does your head ache badly?"

"Not badly."

"Do you want me to close the door?" Laura Linstrom asked as she was going out.

"Please."

The pain that Penny felt was everywhere and nowhere. It was her heart that was sick. Somehow she had been squeezed down into doubt and littleness and did not like herself any more. She did not even want to look out of her own eyes, so she kept them closed.

Penny had not been caught in yesterday's thundershower, but just as she came out of the trees a sulphury finger of lightning had stabbed down at her, and the crash of thunder was so close and loud that it seemed to shatter the world. Poor Benjy jerked and lunged down trail. When Penny looked back the storm cloud had a dark jagged edge, like a tear, where the rain was falling in the high peaks.

"The storm dropped its load up on the rims," Ken said later. "Not enough down here to more than lay the dust."

Ken blamed Bud Lamar for what had happened. Aunt Celia must have told him. "That darned officious kid!" he said. "Takes things into his own hands! Doesn't wait for orders! Well, we're in for it. I can feel it in my bones."

Whatever happened now must logically point to Midnight. Penny herself admitted it. The fear she had felt at the spring was the starkest kind of admission.

Perhaps Ken read her state of mind and chose to spare her further pain, for the subject was dropped. Her mother's solicitousness somehow spotlighted Penny's misery. Only Aunt Celia helped, knitting in the lamplight, saying nothing.

All this morning Penny had lain tensely, listening. Whatever had happened in the night, the herders would know about it and bring in the story. Any moment might bring the news, but by dinner time they would surely know. Noon came and there was no special hum of talk from the dining room. Penny relaxed just a little.

"I do wish you'd let me bring you something to eat," her mother said, putting her hand on Penny's forehead.

"Not yet, Mother. I'm just not hungry. There wasn't any news was there?"

"News, dear? Oh, about your horse. No, no news."

No news was wonderful! The bad kind traveled fast. Men rode any distance to tell it, and those who heard it told it in their turn and rode out to tell it again. Oh, if Midnight came home for his oats tonight and nothing had happened in between . . .

Penny slept. It must have been a long while because the room was dim and there was a late afternoon feeling when she awoke. Almost at once there was a tap at her door and Aunt Celia came in with a small tray.

"I fixed this broth myself," she said, "so you can't politely refuse to taste it. And if you don't eat it all after that I shall be quite insulted!"

"Midnight hasn't come in yet?"

"No, but I have a message for you from that young Bud. He said to tell you your horse's oats and hay are waiting and he's watching so as to close the corral gate the minute he gets back. You look better."

Penny tasted the broth. "It's real good, Auntie!"

"That custard won't hurt you either." Her aunt sat down on the nearest slipper chair. "It's my opinion you've made a life-long friend of a certain young man, the way you handled the affair yesterday. Bud had the look of a devoted St. Bernard when he trusted me with that message for you."

Penny said, "I wonder if he saw Eileen home yesterday."

"Why on earth should he have?"

"Well, Eileen was so upset when she heard Midnight was loose that she wanted Bud to ride home with her. I don't know whether he did, though."

Aunt Celia's laugh was pleasantly dry. "He didn't! I happened to see the Heskett girl riding away by herself. I wondered what had kept her so long. No doubt she tried unsuccessfully to collar young Bud and finally had to brave that mile home by herself!"

Penny said, "The custard is good, too."

"Well, I'm flattered. Will you be down for dinner? *Supper*, as you call it here."

"I do feel a lot better, Auntie, but I won't want any supper after all this!"

Her aunt eyed her for an instant. "If I were you," she said, "I'd get up when I feel like it and not a minute sooner!"

Alone again, it was Bud's voice Penny listened for, an excited call from below her window. The sunset glow on the mountains turned to rose, then violet, tinting her white curtains, then darkened to the shadow-blue of day's end. It was past the time when Midnight normally fed, but Penny still clutched at hope, still listened with all her being.

Full dark now, with no reassuring call from Bud. Midnight had not come. He wasn't going to. Out there on the open range fear and trouble waited.

14

Return in the Night

PENNY HAD LAIN AWAKE WORRYING AND LISTENING FOR HOURS, but she must have slept at last. What wakened her was a fast, light, four-hoof beat—a sound she knew like no other. It was not near at hand, but it was quite distinct in the pre-dawn darkness. The automatic gladness swiftly ebbed as memory returned, the tormenting doubts and fears. Penny got out of bed and went to the window. It was black dark and there was no further sound. If he had gone into the corral the gate must be closed at once and there was no one but her to do it.

Her heart was drumming and her hands shaking as she dressed. There was a moment going down the stairs when she was afraid of the dark itself. The creak of her own footsteps frightened her, but most of all she was afraid of her own crowding thoughts.

The kitchen way was more direct. She was outside now, hurrying through the yard and down past the barn. She heard the nervous blasting of his breath in the dark and paused. The hair stirred on her scalp as she waited.

"Midnight—"

Penny saw him, now, looming against the stars. He was coming toward her. She could not see his eyes. She was afraid, but she willed herself forward.

They met and his head lowered to her, and now what she sensed strongest was *his* fear. Midnight was trembling and quivering under his lathered coat, and his eyes—she could dimly see them in the starlight—were starting with fright. His fear was going through her in a strange way, like the cold fright of a dream.

"You saw something and you ran from it, is that it? You've been running for miles and miles and you're still scared, aren't you?"

Her arm was about his moist neck and the blasting of his breath had become low confiding nickers. They were comforting each other. Slowly, with wonderment and thankfulness, Penny realized that the evil was *outside* of them both. It had gotten into her for a time when faith wavered, but she was free of it now. The truth was so good again. Midnight was a bad horse only to the extent of being willful, a runaway. This was a serious fault and it brought much trouble to them all, but he was not evil. He was good and gentle and loving as she had always known he was.

Penny spoke softly, close to the black ear: "I have to tell you something and you must forgive me. I stopped being afraid *for* you, I was afraid *of* you, and it made me sick. But I'll never, never doubt you again. Whatever comes now we are together against it, not against each other!"

Midnight did forgive her, she knew, but he was still terribly afraid of something out there in the dark. His eyes kept rolling toward the rangeland beyond the corrals.

"What *was* it?" Penny said. "What is it? If you could only tell!"

It was plain that he did not want to go into his own corral.

"The barn then," Penny said. "And I'll light a lantern and rub you down and when you're hungry you can have your oats and hay."

Midnight followed her willingly enough into the barn. Though she still trembled a little, Penny felt delivered. For the moment, at least, it seemed as if she would never be afraid of anything again.

Midnight could not tell her, but as Penny worked over him in the lantern light, rubbing him down, currying his coat, plucking the burrs and foxtails out of his silky mane and tail, some essence of what he knew was conveyed to her, through her sympathy and love, and the fear in him gave way to confidence and calm. From time to time as if remembering, Midnight shivered again, but gradually all tremors ceased and he was cool enough for a long drink and ready for breakfast.

Penny was still busy with him when Sven came out to feed the stock and do the milking. He exclaimed at the sight of her: "You, Miss Penny! What is wrong? Is he hurt?"

"No, Sven, he's all right but something scared him awfully. He came home in a lather and I brought him in here to rub him down."

Sven picked up the lantern and blew it out, then shook it. "A good two hours ago that was!" he said almost accusingly. "I filled this lantern myself only yesterday! Too bad that horse of yours make you so much worry, girl. Too bad!"

"But I *know* something now, Sven!" Penny said. "I'd give anything if I could *prove* it! There's a bad horse out on range but it is *not* Midnight! He's no more to blame for the things that have happened than—than old Huldah!"

"Yah, so," Sven said. His glance at her was heavy and dubious. "Well, it will all come out in the laundry!" he said.

Midnight seemed content to remain in the barn, so Penny left him in his stall and went up to the house. At breakfast she told Ken all about it.

". . . So I think something awful happened last night and Midnight saw it!"

"Wish we could be sure that was *all* he did," Ken said.

"I'm sure, Ken. I was never so sure of anything in my life!"

"Well, too bad, Sis, but it doesn't prove a thing! What you think about that horse carries about as much weight as a doting mother's idea of her only offspring. No matter what he does, including the equivalent of murder, you'll go on believing he's as blameless as the day you first put a rope round his neck."

Vic Corby seemed to see something funny in this and shook with silent mirth.

Somehow Penny could not tell Ken what she had confessed to Midnight, but she told how he had returned in the middle of the night. "Of course, I can't prove what I know, but I know it. I've never seen him so scared. He kept on remembering and shivering for two hours. I think we'll be hearing that another horse was killed last night."

There was general silence and five pairs of eyes came round to Penny. Ken said finally: "Well, Miss Sherlock, how do you deduce that?"

"I'm just sure of it," Penny said. "And Midnight saw it happen, and maybe he was chased by the killer."

"You've got it all worked out, haven't you?" Ken said. "Just the way you want it! Well, we'll hear, never fear!"

It came well before noon. The news was brought by Charlie File whose night camp had been close to the Stoddard line. "There was real ruckusin' on the range last night," Charlie reported. " 'Twas over on Stoddard land this time, not close enough for me to see, but I heard it all, and that scream they tell about. I go along with everything they say about that. If it's a horse, it's a pure maniac. Was I a steer bedded down for the night and heard that screamin', I'd up and high-tail it for Texas. That's just what them Stoddard beeves did, the whole passel of 'em. I got the story from Brick Ennis, one of the Stoddard men. Seems Jake Marlowe was on herd duty at the time. Jake was sittin' by a late fire when he heard that screamin' neigh, first far off, then nearer, and finally the thing busts out of cover, rampin' an' bayin', the black demon hisself. Well, the beeves go plumb crazy, charged right over Jake's fire, Brick says, and like to of tromped him into the ground. Bad hurt, Jake was, had to have the Doc tend him."

Charlie broke off with a sidelong glance at Penny.

"Go on," Ken said.

"Well, I didn't like to say it before, but Brick says Jake got a fair look at that maniac hoss in the moonlight. ' 'Twas that black Midnight hoss of the Linstroms', I'll vow,' Jake said."

"You heard it all, Charlie. What time did it happen?" Penny asked.

"I don't rightly know, Miss Penny. After midnight, it was. One thirty, could of been."

"Well, that wasn't what scared Midnight then," Penny said. "Something else must have happened later."

Ken looked at her and shook his head.

Word of the second incident was brought in by Bud Lamar, who had gone up-country that morning to inspect fences. " 'Twas like Miss Penny said at breakfast," Bud reported in an awed tone. "A horse *was* killed last night. That big gray of the Stoddards', Benbow, 'twas. It happened just a couple of hours before dawn. 'Twas Mr. Stoddard himself told me," Bud said. "His foreman saw the horse that must of done it, a black with a star-mark on his forehead, goin' away from there fast. Claimed 'twas your horse, Miss Penny."

15

The Jekyll
and Hyde Horse

THE NEWSPAPER SOLLY HAD BROUGHT FROM TOWN WAS OPEN
in Aunt Celia's hands and Penny was reading over her
shoulder.

"Right on the first page!" Aunt Celia said.

"I can't imagine who would send that story in to the
paper," Penny's mother said. "It's just a local matter, I
should have thought. No call for the *Brennerton News* to
take it up."

"You forget, Laura. Penny and her horse made the news in Cheyenne. That makes them 'copy,' as they say," said Aunt Celia. "This story has an editorial touch. Someone with a knack for catch phrases."

She was reading aloud now: "'. . . a young girl's gentle, trustworthy pet by day, a rampant terror at night on open range. This Jekyll & Hyde Horse won the hearts of the Frontier Days crowd at Cheyenne, only to return to terrorize the range and kill yet again.' An accomplished tabloid style there, you must admit," Aunt Celia said.

Without warning, Penny burst into tears. "It's a horrible, cruel lie, all of it!" she sobbed. "I wish we could force them to take it all back and apologize."

"Darling," Laura Linstrom said, "everyone knows the ridiculous overstatement of newspaper stories. As Auntie just said the write-up about you in Cheyenne is doubtless responsible for this. Praise, censure, that's the way news goes. We mustn't let it upset us."

"He's *not* a killer! He's not to blame for any of it, but everybody in the country's going to believe the worst about him now! I've got to *do* something about it! I can't just let them think he's an evil horse."

"You're perfectly right, Penny," Aunt Celia said. "You can't just sit! Well, I suggest that you write a letter to the editor. I've known letters to editors to do a lot of good. The editor might even print your letter. That way you have a voice in the matter. The same people who read this piece will most probably read your arguments in Midnight's favor, too."

"That's an excellent suggestion, Penny," her mother said. "Ken's just coming. We'll see what he thinks."

Penny wiped her wet cheeks on her sleeves.

Ken had been the first to see the paper. It was the end of the day and he looked tired and worried, but his eye took in the present situation, taking note also of Penny's reddened eyes. "That story's murder," he said. "I'd like to pistol-whip the responsible party."

"Do sit down, Ken, and try to relax," Laura Linstrom said. "We've just had tea, would you like a cup?"

"No, thanks. I'll have a glass of sherry." Ken sat down with a groan. "All I get from the hands now is 'What's Jekyll & Hyde?'"

"Didn't any of these boys go to school?" Aunt Celia asked. "How do you answer them?"

"I tell them that *The Strange Case of Dr. Jekyll & Mr. Hyde* is a story by Robert Louis Stevenson and to go ahead and read it if they're so interested. I'll bet there'll be a run on the book at the Brennerton library at that. . . . No use crying about it, Penny, it's done."

"Celia has just made a very good suggestion," Laura said. "We want to know what you think. She says that a letter from Penny to the editor refuting his statements and presenting arguments in Midnight's favor might do considerable good."

"Fine," Ken said, "but she's not in a position to refute anything. If that horse had been *in* just one of these times I'd go to bat on it myself. But we have nothing to go on. The same black horse was involved each time, they've got that pretty well established. And Midnight was not only loose but seen. They've got their case, Auntie. We might as well face the facts."

"They're *not* the facts," Penny said.

Ken shrugged. "We all know how you feel, Sweets. It's too bad."

"Well, a letter to the editor most certainly won't do any harm," Laura said.

Penny spent the evening at the small French desk in her room, struggling with words. She spent most of the following morning there, too, and her wastebasket was full of crumpled paper, unsuccessful attempts to express her surging thoughts. The more she wrote about Midnight's nobility, the more Dr. Jekyllish it sounded, and that meant Mr. Hyde was just around the corner, waiting to show his ugly face. She couldn't seem to make her argument convincing and her story of Midnight's two and a half years of life, his gentle heart and quick intelligence sounded as biased as Ken insisted it was.

At last Penny admitted to herself that she could not write this letter. She didn't care so much what those Brennerton people thought anyway. What she did care about was their neighbors, people who knew her and knew her horse. If she could just talk to them and tell them the things she had tried to write.

Why not call and talk to them direct? She would visit one and all of the surrounding ranches and make her appeal first hand. Of course she would ride Midnight, so he would be there for people to see. He always made a wonderful impression. Surely anyone who looked him in the eye would be convinced in a way that a whole book of letters to the editor could not bring about.

Penny told no one what she intended to do. Sometimes people's thoughts weakened one's resolve, and for what she now planned she needed to be strong and unswerving. To Penny it would be a crusade. When you felt very strongly about some cause and were bent on telling others about it so they would believe in it, too, you were a crusader.

Penny groomed her horse, dressed neatly and set out. At first she thought of going direct to the Heskett ranch where the trouble and the stories had started. But the Stoddards had fared even worse, what with the injury to Jake Marlowe. One probably ought to start by going there and inquiring how Jake was. On the other hand, she should be very sure of herself when she went there. She wasn't yet. She felt strongly about it but her words might stumble—or fail her utterly!

Start with the Tillotsons, she thought. Their holdings were smaller and farther away. The Tillotsons were scarcely to be called neighbors, but in the high range country all within a radius of fifteen miles were still neighbors. In the old days they had not only been neighbors but one big family, her father used to say. People living as far as six hundred miles apart read the Cheyenne newspaper and kept track of each other through its statewide personal columns.

The Tillotson ranch house had a long ell at the rear that had been the original log cabin, and the house was completely surrounded by a pole fence. Penny left Midnight at the hitching rack and went in through the gate, announced by two friendly mongrels with hair in their eyes like sheep dogs. She went to the front door and hesitated, somehow aware that this entrance was seldom used. There were stirrings within before the door was opened by Mrs. Tillotson herself with her apron in her hands and a starey look of surprise on her nice broad face. Penny told them who she was and was invited to sit down.

"You maybe come from the Red Cross or the church?" Mrs. Tillotson asked.

"Oh, no, I'm not soliciting!"

"Oh, you visit us. Nice!" Mrs. Tillotson's smile broadened till it crinkled and all but closed her blue eyes. "Cecie! Nora!" she called. "We've got company!"

Now two young women came into the parlor, nodding and smiling, each with a baby in her arms and small children walking behind. These were Mrs. Tillotson's daughters-in-law who lived with her, their husbands working the ranch with their father. Soon a tray with coffee and sweet rolls was brought in and it was like a party, all talking at once and loudly, above the excited squeals of the children.

Penny was having a delightful time, but what of her purpose? How could she even speak of it now? But somehow she must, or fail Midnight and her cause.

The moment came when Mrs. Tillotson spoke of the "Phantom Black Horse" that was making so much trouble for the ranchers "over south." Had they, the Linstroms, been plagued by it?

"No, we haven't," Penny said. "Only the Hesketts and Stoddards have reported any real trouble, but there are lots and lots of stories about a black mystery horse and it is a very great worry to me. You see, my horse is black and sometimes he gets loose for a day or two. Some of the herders have seen him out on range, or thought they did, and they are blaming him for the trouble. It's just a terrible mistake, because my horse couldn't be gentler or more obedient—"

The three women clucked and murmured indignantly: "Your horse, Miss Linstrom? Of course he would be gentle and kind! Why should folks blame him? Ah well, that is the way such things go! The innocent must suffer for the guilty one! But *that one!* He is a very demon! He kills horses and cattle, and he would kill men, too, if he could! Some herders, they say, only escaped by the grace of God! We have been expecting him to strike at our place, and Papa and the boys are on the lookout day and night . . ."

Penny felt stunned at this additional evidence of how rumor grew and spread. "I don't think it is nearly as bad as they say," she said at last. "Before I go I would like you to see my horse. I'm sure you can tell by looking at him that he would never do any of those things."

16

Penny's Crusade

AT LEAST SOME OF THE RANCH FOLK HAD READ THE DOCTOR
Jekyll and Mr. Hyde story, because on the Starbuck ranch,
which Penny visited next, this was what she heard:

"A dolly-hoss and a killer, all t'once, from what I hear.
Never heard tell of such a combination before, outside of a
book. Seems like the Old Nick don't break out in the critter
'til it gets dark. And then it's hunt your hole for man or
beast."

It was Mr. Starbuck himself who was speaking. He was an elderly man with a reputation as a horse trader, who had come to Wyoming from New Hampshire in his early years. Penny remembered that her father had always admired Mr. Starbuck's "horse sense" and had had dealings with him a number of times.

"Mr. Starbuck," Penny said now, "you know horses better than most anyone around here, I know. My father used to say you could tell a horse's age and disposition at a glance, without looking at his mouth or trying him out. I remember the blue *grullo* he bought from you. The best cutting horse he ever owned, Dad always said."

Penny had Mr. Starbuck's full attention now. He was fingering his gray wispy beard and eyeing her speculatively.

"I've brought my own horse over for you to look at, Mr. Starbuck. You know they're calling him a lot of bad names just now and putting all the blame on him for what's been happening out on range. But he's a good, gentle horse and you will judge him without any prejudice, I know."

"Hm-m," Mr. Starbuck said.

"Perhaps Mrs. Starbuck and the girls would like to see him, too," Penny added.

The family had received her cordially and she had sat on the shaded porch with them, drinking lemonade and talking of indifferent matters before the subject of the "Night Screamer" came up. Unlike the Tillotsons, Mr. Starbuck was well aware that her horse was suspect, but no more than they, it seemed, did he question the authenticity of the stories going round.

All four of the Starbucks now accompanied Penny to the hitching rack to look Midnight over. Mr. Starbuck had never seen her horse before, Penny was sure. For a long moment he said nothing, just gave Midnight his measured appraisal while the girls and Mrs. Starbuck exclaimed how pretty he was, and said who would think a handsome horse like that would turn out so mean.

Penny was waiting tensely for Mr. Starbuck's judgment. "Well, you could fool me with that one, goin' and comin'," he said. "I'd a took him for *saddle horse* pure an' simple! Quietest, best-mannered, willingest horse you could hope to see! High fire, yes, more energy than a stiff day's climb could take the cream off of. A mite too much ginger, could be. Kill himself for you though, in the manner of his kind. Take longer doing it, that's all." Mr. Starbuck turned away, head shaking. "Enough to make a man mistrust his own intelleck!" he said. "Fooled!"

Penny was almost in tears. "But Mr. Starbuck, you're not fooled! You read him like a book! He's just the way you said, just the way he *looks!* My father gave him to me when he was a month old. I've trained him and taken care of him ever since and I've never known him to do a mean or an 'ornery' thing in his whole life! He's considerate and gentle and obedient always. He wants to be just super and that's what he is!"

Mr. Starbuck was weighing her with his fine-gauge horse-trader's eye. "Well," he said finally, "this super horse of yours has gone an' got himself into the worst mess of repute an animal ever called down!"

"But he hasn't really, Mr. Starbuck. It's all a big mistake."

"Your horse has been seen, ain't he, girl? Two-three times right at the time an' place of the scurvy doin's. Caught red-handed, as you might say."

"There's some other black horse, Mr. Starbuck, there must be! Midnight does get loose now and then. People may see him, of course, but he's not the black they tell about. He's not a killer. He's never had so much as a bite on him, and he just couldn't fight two other stallions to death without there being some sign."

Mr. Starbuck shook his head. "With this critter there ain't nothing but contradictions. Another black, you say. There ain't no other black around here—'cepting Shiloh, and he's never loose. Used to be that wild Wapiti stallion back in the hills. Years ago that was. He ain't been seen or heard from, and this here fellow has."

Penny tried once more. "You know at night any dark horse looks black. It could be a roan or a chestnut!"

"Black's black," Mr. Starbuck said.

Penny was beaten. He hadn't given an inch, yet all through their talk his eye kept going back to Midnight with a horseman's glow of appreciation.

If a man who knew horses wouldn't believe his own eyes, what could you do? It must mean that people liked these evil stories better than the truth. Yet there was nothing to do but finish what she had begun.

It was still fairly early when she left the Starbucks. The way home led near the Heskett ranch and there was time for an afternoon call. She had been waiting for this visit until she felt a little surer of herself, but there was no use putting it off any longer. She turned in at the Hesketts' poplar-shaded lane and rode up to the prosperous-looking two-story ranch house. The Heskett house dog was a Chihuahua named Tito. His shrill barking brought Eileen to the door. She stopped short, staring, mouth agape.

"Why, Penny Linstrom, you're the last person in the world I expected to see!"

"Were you expecting someone else?" Penny asked.

"Well, no, come on in, Penny. That is, not exactly. Pres Hiller said he might drop around this afternoon. Say, how did you get here?" Eileen was peering out the door. "What? Don't tell me you rode that brute over here!"

"Don't be silly," Penny said. "Of course I rode him over!"

"Well, my gosh, I hope you tied him well. Bob's favorite buckskin is in the field just across the lane."

Penny controlled herself. "Midnight is not going to break away, Eileen, and he wouldn't do any harm if he did."

"Oh, no, not much! He just about killed Jake Marlowe, that's all!"

Penny felt tired all at once. "You know perfectly well that it was the stampeding stock that did that!"

"Yes, but it was that horse's fault!"

"Jake Marlowe is getting better, isn't he?"

"Oh, sure, he'll live! Come on upstairs, Penny, I've got some stuff to show you. We can keep an eye on that horse of yours from my window."

Penny had hoped to talk with the elder Hesketts and perhaps get in a word or two in Midnight's behalf, but no one else was about, so she followed Eileen upstairs and sat on her friend's flowered cretonne spread, looking at pretty new clothes. Such an array: formals and informals, sports and loungewear.

"Are you going away to school this fall?" Penny asked.

"No. Why?"

"Well, all these clothes! As if you were starting college or getting married or something!"

Eileen smiled sweetly: "You know I don't graduate from Brennerton High till year after next! I have to have a few clothes, though. I go out a lot."

Now Penny had Eileen's snapshot album in her lap and it was all Eileen: in tennis shorts, in a bathing suit, in jodhpurs and white Stetson, in billowy peasant skirt, street wear, formal, all posed against the painted clapboard wall of the ranch house.

"Oh, don't bother looking at those old things, Penny! Toward the back—*here!*—are some of Pres—"

Penny knew Pres Hiller, a sophomore at Brennerton High whose father ran a grocery store in town.

"Pres is cute, don't you think so?" Eileen said. "*That* one was down at Bass Lake two-three weeks ago. This was the same day. We were wrestling and Ella Barnes snapped us—"

There was a third picture of Eileen riding Pres' shoulders, both in bathing suits and Pres looking close to collapse.

"Say, what about you and that Bud Lamar?"

"Nothing about Bud and me!" Penny said.

"Oh, well, if that's the way you feel about it! I thought we were buddies. There's Bob down there looking at your horse," Eileen said a moment later, looking out the window. "Hey, Bob, do you know what horse that is?"

"I was wondering," her brother called back. "Is Penny Linstrom up there?"

"That's right, she's here. So now you know! Better watch out!"

"Jeepers!" Bob flung up an arm and staggered backwards in a pantomime of terror. "Hi, Penny, how's kicks?" he called up.

"I have to go now, Eileen," Penny said.

"Aw, why? You just got here and you hardly ever come."

When the two girls went downstairs Mrs. Heskett was in the sitting room with Margie, who was eight. Bob came inside.

"My favorite blonde!" Bob said.

"What do you think, Mom, Penny rode all the way over here on *that* horse!" Eileen said. "And you worry if I'm a few minutes late when I'm riding Patchy!"

Mrs. Heskett was the worrying kind. It showed in her smileless gray eyes and turned down lips. "I just haven't had a moment's peace since this trouble began," she said. "I never know what's going to happen next!"

Penny spoke out: "Mrs. Heskett, my horse has had no more to do with what's been happening than Patchy!"

"Can you prove that?" Bob asked.

"I'm sure it *will* be proved!" Penny said.

"It'll take some doing, Beautiful. That horse of yours has been seen all over the place, and every time things happen you folks have to admit that he's loose!"

In defense of her horse, Penny could only tell once again how Midnight had come home lathered from running and trembling with fright the night the Stoddard horse was killed. "There were no marks of a fight on him, but I think he was chased."

Bob said: "I might buy that if there was another black horse hereabouts." He laughed: "Could be it was his own conscience scared him so."

17

The Lonely Clearing

PENNY HAD MADE SOME TACTFUL INVESTIGATIONS, BUT IF THERE was another black horse loose on range, his owner was guarding his secret well. Penny chose a Sunday afternoon for her visit to the Stoddard ranch. She found both Mr. and Mrs. Stoddard at home, but felt at once the difference in them, a tinge of coolness, as though they were offended somehow and expected an apology. When she inquired about Jake Marlowe, Mr. Stoddard said:

"Oh, Jake's coming along all right, but I've lost a lot of man-hours, to say nothing of my horse."

"I'm sorry you think my horse is responsible, Mr. Stoddard," Penny said. "I'm sure he is not, but so far I haven't been able to prove that there's another black horse making all the trouble."

"No, and you'll have a hard time doing it, girl," Mr. Stoddard said sourly.

"There is, though," Penny said. "There has to be. I've been trying to find out something about Pitchdark, the Wapiti stallion we used to hear so much about."

Mr. Stoddard snorted. "It's a question in my mind if there ever was such a critter! Years ago it was a wild *white* stallion they talked about. 'A milk-white pacer with coal-black ears,' they said. 'Wild as the wind, fast as light.' The 'Ghost Horse,' he was called, and 'The Phantom White.' Everybody and his uncle wanted that horse. Every trick was tried to catch him—running him down, walking him down, creasing, roping, penning him. Never was caught. I'd need a whole lot of proof that white feller ever existed, too!"

"I'm sure Pitchdark existed," Penny said. "My father saw him once with his mares in the Wapiti foothills. But you are right. When stories like these get started they go on and on and grow and grow, whether they're true or not."

She had made her point. For an instant both Mr. and Mrs. Stoddard had a cornered look. Penny followed it up.

"When such stories are about your own horse, and you *know* they're not true, it's pretty hard to stand. That's why I wanted to talk to you about it and have you look at him. If a horse is mean you can tell by his eyes. Don't you agree with me, Mr. Stoddard?"

"General thing, yes."

They both went with her to look at Midnight, and Mr. Stoddard said, "Right handsome beast, no denyin' that. But no denyin' what my herders seen neither."

This was the same offended tone and look she had met when she came. Failure again. Nothing but failure from the start. But telling Mr. Stoddard about her father's having seen Pitchdark had stirred up other memories and freshened her hope again.

There was a man who lived in the back hills that her father used to visit and sometimes he had taken her along. Dolf Arneson, his name was, an old friend of Carl Linstrom's and a natural born horseman, her father used to say. Penny remembered the delicious pastries Mrs. Arneson used to serve with coffee. As they sat in the Arnesons' kitchen the talk of the two men would invariably come back to the Wapiti stallion. Once Mr. Arneson had told them how the beautiful wild black had come right down to his place to drink. He had seen him at his salt lick and followed him and his band up into the high hills. It was on a ride with Mr. Arneson that her father had seen Pitchdark with his own eyes. Why hadn't she thought of Dolf Arneson before?

The last few years of his life Carl Linstrom had stopped visiting the Arnesons. Penny did not know why. She had heard of Mrs. Arneson's death and that their daughter had married and gone away. Mr. Arneson must be a very lonely man these days.

The day after her Stoddard visit, Penny started up-country to call on her father's old friend. The Arneson homestead was a six mile ride from Paintrock, up near Moon Creek, and Penny started soon after midday. Beyond the grasslands the trail wound up through scrubby juniper and pinon pine. Sheep country, the cattlemen called this. Penny remembered that there was nothing but sheep spreads above the Arnesons', though Dolf himself had raised cattle and horses. How long had it been since she rode this trail with her father? The way seemed altered, stonier and bleaker, and where was the stream? Quite clearly she remembered a long pleasant stretch of willow shade with trout pools and shallows where one's horse might drink and wade. Now there was only the stream bed itself, bleached and stony, and the standing sticks of dead willows. Nowhere had the drought struck so deeply as here, Penny thought. The massive cliffs above her had a forbidding look. Suddenly, the impulse was upon her to turn back. But she pressed on. If anyone would know about Pitchdark, it would be Dolf Arneson.

A broken-down pole fence and a disused shed were the first signs of human habitation. Things looked vaguely familiar, yet Penny could not believe this was the Arneson place, remembering how neat and orderly it had always been. Her father had admired the old-world charm of the log house with its stone fireplace, hand-hewn furniture and wood carvings Dolf had fashioned in the long winter days.

Now Penny rounded a turn in the trail into the Arneson clearing. Weather-worn and darkened the cabin might well have been, but not so sagging and neglected looking as this, with panes missing in the windows and chinking gone from between the logs. It looked abandoned, yet at the same time you knew that it was occupied. It seemed to Penny that she felt eyes watching as she approached.

Midnight was acting very nervous. He whinnied and there came an answer from somewhere behind the cabin. Instead of dropping the reins to the ground as usual, Penny tied him securely to a tree branch.

"Mr. Arneson," she called out.

There was no answer. Penny went up to the split-log door-step and knocked at the heavy old door. She continued to knock, confident that he was there and must finally show himself.

Abruptly the door swung wide. The man who confronted her was not holding a rifle in his hands, but the effect was the same. His whole attitude was that of one facing an ene-my. How terribly thin he was, and his eyes were the saddest she had ever seen. Penny would scarcely have recognized him with his scraggly beard, except for his unusual height, which she remembered. The silence atop that gaunt, six-foot-four frame seemed a mixture of challenge and accusation.

For a moment Penny was too startled to speak.

"Mr. Arneson, I don't suppose you remember me."

As if that were self-evident, he stood there staring at her.

"I'm Penny—Penny Linstrom. I used to visit you with my father when I was little."

Still the man did not answer or move and scarcely seemed to register her words.

"You remember my father, Mr. Arneson? Carl Linstrom?"

When she spoke the name it was like striking spark from stone. "Once he was my friend, but he stopped being friend."

So there had been trouble of some sort between Dolf and her father. That was why those visits had stopped four or five years ago. Penny could only hope that her father had had nothing to do with the darkening of Dolf Arneson's life or the saddening of his eyes. It was not in Carl Linstrom's character to do so, so far as she knew.

"My father was not the kind of man to stop being a friend," she said.

"With me he did more than stop. He turned against his friend."

The shock of this stopped Penny for a moment, for there might be fanaticism, but there was no lie in those sad eyes.

"Mr. Arneson," she said, "you must be mistaken. My father was a good man, too. He always liked you, I know it, and he was a countryman of yours. If there was something he did wrong he would want to make it right. He was killed in an accident last year, so he cannot act for himself. But I can act for him. Please tell me what happened."

She got no intelligible reply. Instead the man seemed suddenly beside himself, ranting incoherently. He seemed to be talking about the land drying up and stock dying before it could be sold.

"When you rob a man of his water, you take his life's blood. Might as well you murder him!"

Surely Mr. Arneson had brooded overmuch up here in this lonely cabin. Grief and hardship and loneliness had taken too deep a toll.

"A drought year like this is hard on all of us, Mr. Arneson," Penny said. "What I wanted to ask is whether you know anything about Pitchdark, the wild stallion that used to range these hills. The Wapiti Stallion everybody called him. You and my father used to talk about him. Pitchdark used to come down to your salt lick. Down our way no one seems to have heard anything about him the last few years."

"Who sent you?" Arneson asked suspiciously. "Who wants to know?"

"No one sent me, but I need help, Mr. Arneson. My horse is in bad trouble. Down on the range things have been happening lately. Fences broken and cattle stampeded and two young stallions killed by a black horse that was seen several times. My horse is black and the ranchers are blaming him. I know he's not the one, but I must prove it. There must be another black horse loose on range. Can you tell me anything about Pitchdark, Mr. Arneson?"

"I have nothing to tell."

This final disappointment Penny could hardly accept.

"Do you suppose Pitchdark is dead then?"

Dolf Arneson gave a shrug. "Who knows? Maybe your horse is a bad one," he said, "maybe not. It's nothing to me. You've come to the wrong place for help."

The animosity back of his words frightened Penny. Whatever it was that was wrong, Dolf Arneson wanted it to stay that way. The feeling upon Penny as she rode away was that this man had learned to hate deeply, and could not stop it, did not want to. Once more she was beaten, and her crusade for Midnight was at an end.

18

A Ride Together

PENNY WAS RIDING SLOWLY PAST THE WHITE FENCED MEADOWS and corrals of the Armstrong place, so compact and neat and totally different from a cattle ranch. In one fenced pasture were two thoroughbred mares and their awkward leggy foals. Whinnying briskly, Midnight was answered from many quarters, even from the rear stockades where Shiloh was kept. All this horse talk might bring someone out, Penny thought. She hoped it would bring Russ. She hesitated to call at the house and disturb him at his work, but she did need help, the kind of help that Russ alone could give. For only he in the whole world, it seemed, had the implicit belief in Midnight that she had.

Penny had finally told her mother and aunt about visiting the neighbors, and Aunt Celia said it was a much better idea than writing to the paper. Even if she had not convinced folks that her horse was guiltless, the effort she had made would surely tell. Mother did not say much, but her smile was approving. After talking the matter over the three of them decided against telling Ken about the visits. There was nothing reassuring to report and Ken had more than enough to bother him. Penny wished she could ask her brother if he knew of any trouble between their father and Dolf Arneson, but then she would have to tell him about her call up there and all the rest of it. The visit to Dolf Arneson Penny had not mentioned at all. The man's strange antipathy and the pain and injury she had sensed in him had disturbed her so that she kept it secret.

Penny could see the Armstrong ranch house now, painted red with a white trim. She had about made up her mind to go in and ask for Russ when she saw him coming on foot along the drive.

"Hi, Penny!" he called.

"I just wondered if you were going out for a ride this afternoon!"

"Good idea," Russ said. "Are you coming in?"

"No, I'll just wait . . . if you're coming."

"Okay. Right with you."

The mere sight of Russ made Penny feel better about things. In a corral farther along, four yearlings were frisking. One of them, a bay with white feet, was remarkably fast, it seemed to her. She remarked about this when Russ joined her on Janus.

"That's Dad's pet, too," Russ said. "Dad's banking on that boy. Penny, I wish you'd ride round this way oftener! It'd be a real favor to me. There I was up to my eyes in old cases when I start hearing horse hellos all over the place and look out the window and there you are!"

"I was thinking about coming in," Penny said, "but I was afraid you'd be in the midst."

"In-the-midst, that's me! You're a lifesaver, no fooling!"

This was wonderful to hear. Somehow Russ always said just the right nice things. Walking their horses and talking, Penny felt too cheerful to bring up the matters that had been troubling her. It was Russ who opened the subject with mention of the piece in the *Brennerton News.*

" 'Jekyll and Hyde horse!' It made me sore. Why can't people just mind their own business?"

"I guess it's because they don't have enough to talk about," Penny said. "When they get hold of something interesting they won't give it up! I've been finding that out lately, calling on our neighbors—"

She was telling him the whole story, from the Tillotsons to the Stoddards, and how everyone she talked to had something to add to the original lurid tale about *that* horse: Mrs. Tillotson's declaring that he killed cattle and horses and would kill men, too, if he got the chance, and Mr. Starbuck saying it was enough to make a man "mistrust his own in-telleck" because Midnight looked and acted like the best of saddle horses.

Russ had to laugh, but his look showed genuine concern.

"Worse than I thought," he said. "One of those things that start the size of a snowball and turn into an avalanche. And not a grain of truth in the whole."

Penny drew a deep breath of gratitude and relief.

"That's why I rode over to your house today, Russ, just to hear you say something like that! You're about the last person I know who believes in Midnight any more."

"Believe in him! I know him! If 'Night had the kind of bad in him they're talking about we'd have found it out long ago."

It made Penny ashamed to remember her own doubts and fears. When she told Russ about Midnight's terror the night of the second horse-killing he said, "That sure argues for another black horse out on range."

"I know it does," Penny said, "but if anyone knows about another black horse they're not saying, not even Dolf Arne-son."

She had not meant to let the name slip out.

"Dolf Arneson? He's still living out there on Moon Creek, isn't he? What were you doing up there?"

"Well, the reason I went up there was to ask about Pitch-dark," Penny said. "My father and Dolf Arneson used to be friends. In the old days Mr. Arneson seemed to know more about Pitchdark than anyone else. But the other day when I asked him, he said he had nothing to tell. He said I'd come to the wrong place for help!"

"Nice friendly guy!" Russ said.

"He used to be nice, though, really Russ! In the old days they were a very nice family. Dad used to go up there every once in a while and take me with him."

"In the old days!" Russ grinned at her. "Sounds about forty years ago! When was it, about?"

"Four or five years ago," Penny said. "And then all at once Dad stopped going."

"Know why?" Russ asked.

"No—no, I don't know why."

"Did you tell Arneson why you were so interested in Pitchdark?"

"Yes, I said Midnight was being blamed just because he was a black horse."

"Did he act sympathetic at all?"

"Well, no. He said maybe my horse was a bad one and maybe not, it was nothing to him. It's not a bit like the way he used to be, Russ! He was a nice man, really. But his wife died and things happened. He's had a lot of trouble."

"Sure must have," Russ said.

Moments later he was still thinking about it. "I think I know that Arneson on sight," he said. "Extra tall, isn't he?"

"Yes, and terribly skinny. He's bearded and has very sad eyes. Actually, he looks as if he were starving. Could he be that poor, I wonder?"

"Could be, of course. Look, Penny, I don't think you ought to go up in that sheep country alone. It's not too safe. If you have to go up there again for any reason, let me know and I'll ride along."

They had come to a stream called The Snake and dismounted to let the horses drink.

"I can't remember ever seeing this creek so low," Russ said.

"Moon Creek's completely dry," Penny said. "It has changed the whole look of things up there. Even the willows are dead."

"Willows don't die in one season," Russ said. "I think the drought's going to break soon, though. Sort of feel it in my bones."

"I hope your bones are right," Penny said. "I think this weather is partly to blame for all the trouble. Russ, did you really mean that about my riding over oftener?"

"I sure did," Russ said. "Now that Denver's less than a month away I feel as if I'd been missing out on the whole summer and it gets me down."

She would be careful not to abuse the privilege, Penny thought, but how good to know that she could interrupt Russ' studies when the need was real. As they rode on again Penny was happier than she had been since the last day at Cheyenne.

19

High-Country Storm

"HELP YOURSELF, BUD," KEN SAID, GIVING THE BOY A SECOND, sharper glance.

Penny, too, was attentive. Bud had been out on herd duty last night and he had news—his very pores exuded excitement—but right now he was filling his plate with meat. In the first lull in the table talk it came out:

"Boy! Mr. Linstrom! Miss Penny! The Black Screamer of the hills was sure loose again last night!"

147

Penny's first reaction was one of shock. Her nerves tautened and her skin prickled from sheer habit. Then it dawned
on her that this might well be the news they had hoped for
so long, because Midnight had been in last night and they
could prove it.

Ken seemed quite as electrified as she, waiting tensely for
the boy to go on, but Bud had taken too big a bite of hot
potato and was blowing on it. All present were waiting now.
Solly said, "That's our boy! Get us all going like this, then
stuffs his mouth so he can't talk. All we need now is for
Buddie-boy to choke to death on that and leave us all guess-
in' forever."

"Where was the 'Black Screamer' seen, Bud?" Ken asked.

"On Stoddard land again 'twas, Mr. Linstrom! This time
Link Joslin was on night watch, but I didn't talk to Link
himself. First I knowed was when Ed Sanders come noseyin'
his buckskin over my way as I'm headin' home this mornin'.
Ten, it might of been, or a mite better. I knew right away
he had somethin' to tell."

"Yes, yes, we know it, too!" Ken said impatiently. "But
what?"

Penny was breathless with suspense.

"Well, first thing Ed asks is, 'You hear anything queer last
night?' I didn't say right off. I let on like I might of and then
again I might not. Well, that's when he come out with it.
'The Black Screamer of the Hills was out again last night
with maybe the devil himself a-ridin' him!' Ed's just had it
from Link. 'An' I suppose Link says it was Miss Penny's
horse he saw!' I says to Ed. 'You're tootin' right he did! Same

black horse as always, a-rampin' and ruckusin' like that Headless Hossman the ha'nt tales tell about. Me, I'm stayin' in the bunkhouse from now on, sundown till sunup,' Ed says. Well, I laughed in his face. 'Miss Penny's horse was t'home last night,' I says. 'Has been for a week and more.' 'You shore of that?' Ed says. 'Shore I'm shore, an' there's eight-nine other people to back me up on it!'" Bud leaned back and beamed round the table.

"What *happened?*" Ken said again. "What's the *story?* Any fences broken, herd scattered, horses killed?"

"That's the funny part of it," Bud said. "Soon as I mentioned Midnight was in, Ed sort of backed off from the whole thing. 'Reckon Link must of had himself a nightmare!' Ed said. 'Or else he made it up out o' whole cloth!' And Ed just turned and rode off."

Ken dropped his head into his hands and groaned aloud. Solly sighed at his plate, one lean hand flapping hopelessly in air.

"Oh, Bud, if you'd just let him talk first!" Penny said. "*Before* you told him Midnight was in!"

"Gee, Miss Penny, I never thought of that! I just figured this once we had it on 'em—"

"And we had—for the first time!" Ken said. "But Bud, you sure goofed it up! If you'd given Ed Simms a chance to get that story out we'd have something to quote back at them."

Bud's prideful look had collapsed into embarrassment and dismay.

"Anyway," Penny said, "it proves there is another horse making trouble and that's something."

"It might have proved something," Ken said. "As it is, they'll just call Link Joslin a liar and let it go at that."

Solly excused himself and left the table, pieless and muttering. A moment later he looked in at the door again.

"Young Armstrong just rode up," he said. "Asking for you, Miss Penny."

"Thank you, Solly."

"Do ask Russell to come in," Laura Linstrom called.

"I will, Mother." Penny was already running out the door.

It was only the day before yesterday that they had seen each other last, and here he was on Janus asking if she would like to ride up-country with him this afternoon.

"I've been thinking over what you told me about that Dolf Arneson," Russ said. "Strikes me that fellow knows a lot more about the Wapiti stallion than he lets on. Anyway, I'd like to ask him a few questions myself."

Penny asked Russ to come in while she got ready, adding in an undertone: "But please don't say anything about Dolf Arneson. You're the only one I've told about going up there."

She left Russ in the dining room talking to the family and went to change. It seemed as if things were really beginning to break for Midnight at last—Bud's exciting news, even if it turned out disappointingly, and now Russ' sudden feeling about Dolf Arneson. Once Russ' interest was caught his mind went on burrowing till he got to the very bottom of things! If anyone could solve this mystery it would be Russ.

When she joined them all again, Russ and Aunt Celia were chatting together and Penny could tell that her aunt was quite taken with him.

"Russell says the ride you are planning will take the whole afternoon," Laura Linstrom said, "and he's agreed to come back and have supper with us."

The afternoon was muggy and warm.

There was a bank of dark cloud hanging over the Elkhorn rims. Ordinarily this would mean rain for later in the day, but this year all signs failed.

"Did they tell you the news Bud Lamar brought in?" Penny asked as they rode. "Another black horse out there making trouble last night, with Midnight safe at home! That's the best news in the world! If only Bud had let Ed Simms finish what he had to say we might know something."

"Too bad it was Link Joslin's story," Russ said. "I don't know him too well myself, but Jake says he'll tell any kind of tall tale to get some excitement going."

"Just the same," Penny said, "I have a feeling something's going to break!"

"I think we're on the track of something right now," Russ said. "The idea's been growing on me ever since we talked. Did Arneson act suspicious when you spoke of Pitchdark?"

"Well, yes, he asked who sent me."

"How did you answer that, Penny?"

"I said no one had sent me. That was when I said I needed his help about Pitchdark, if he knew anything."

"And that was when he said you'd come to the wrong place for help," Russ said. "Your impression was that he hates the whole world—that sort of attitude?"

"Well, he acted that way," Penny said. "He's certainly been hurt badly by something."

Penny's eyes were on the slopes beyond and above. Even from this distance she could make out the winding bed of Moon Creek, a bleached gray vein on the mountainside. She did not like to speak of Arneson's trouble with her father, but very likely Russ would get it out of her anyway. He was a lawyer already the way he put his questions.

"I wonder why your father liked the guy," Russ said next.

Penny sighed. "I might as well tell you everything! There must have been some trouble between them—I don't know what! But when I spoke my father's name he flared up and said Dad had turned against him! I asked what the trouble was but he wouldn't say."

"Your father wouldn't turn against him for nothing! That goes right along with my feeling that Arneson is hiding something. Try to remember anything else he said that might give us a clue."

"Well, he said some wild things about *water*," Penny said. "I thought he was talking about the drought. He said if you rob a man of his water you take his life's blood. You might as well murder him, he said. He didn't speak clearly, I could hardly understand, but he acted angry and accusing."

"Well, for gosh sake!" Russ said. "Water might be a clue at that. Say, look at those clouds over the peak. If it's drought he was talking about, looks like he'll have relief real soon!"

They were on a steep grade now. Ahead of them a curtain of dark vapor was lowering. Penny watched it slowly blotting out the rock masses to their right. It seemed to flow down over the pines like soft gray wax. Both horses were jittery. Probably they ought to turn back, she thought, but it was the last thing she wanted to do and she hoped Russ wouldn't suggest it. Russ' next words showed that his thoughts were miles away:

"Water," he said reflectively. "Seems to me I remember something about Moon Creek water, several years back, but I was too young to be interested. I'll ask Dad if he knows anything about it."

Around a bend in the trail Penny saw the broken-down fence and disused shed that marked the beginning of the Arneson clearing. "We're almost there," she said, feeling depressed as before by the dilapidation of the once neat homestead.

"Looks deserted," Russ said as they came in sight of the cabin.

"It did to me before, too, but Mr. Arneson was there," Penny said.

They dismounted. "If that storm breaks, the horses may give us a little trouble," Russ said. "Better tie them."

"Midnight hates thunder," Penny said.

Together they went up to the split-log doorstep and Russ knocked. No sound from within. This time Penny had the feeling that there would be no answer, that even if Mr. Arneson was there he would give no sign.

"I'll try once more," Russ said and laid on his knuckles in a resounding knock. It echoed hollowly, emptily. "Well, we're out of luck. Wow, look at it now!"

The dark clouds had swept down in the sudden way of high country storms and were literally swirling about them. Leading the horses, they moved round to the corral at the rear of the cabin. It was empty, but showed that one or more horses had been there earlier in the day.

"Might find him somewhere up-trail," Russ said. "Let's ride along a ways and see."

Above the cabin, rickety old fences and cattle pens showed that no stock had been kept there for a long time. Further along, the trail dipped into a pine-clad valley.

"Fresh horse tracks all along here," Russ said. "Maybe he went that-a-way—" He pointed down toward the vapor-wrapped pines.

Midnight was blowing and fidgeting worse than before and Janus was nervous too. Penny did not want to go down this trail. She was actually afraid, though for no reason that she could have named.

"Looks like my hunch to come up here has thrown us for a loss," Russ said. "We'd better head back."

Just before they reached the clearing again the mountain storm broke with furious gusts of wind and rain and thunder-claps that set both horses dancing in terror. Penny was glad she had her leather jumper.

"That old shed we saw on the way in!" Russ shouted. "Let's make for it, but fast! We can wait there till the worst is over—"

The shed was certainly their best bet. By the time they reached it the storm was a near cloudburst and the mountain world rocked with flares and crashes.

20

The Phantom Screamer

THE STORM HAD SETTLED INTO A STEADY RAIN AND DAY WAS ending when Penny and Russ started down trail. A sense of uneasiness had been growing on Penny as they waited with the horses in the shed. She thought that it must leave her now, starting home, but the apprehension grew as they rode. Midnight shared her sense of foreboding, Penny was sure. Russ, too, seemed intent on leaving this dreary, shadowed place.

155

"Too bad it happened this way," he said. "Hope you don't catch cold."

"Oh, I won't," Penny said. "We're going to be late for supper, though. Russ, is there a creepy feeling up here, or am I just imagining it?"

"It's plenty crawly," Russ said. "I'll be glad when we're out of it."

"I wish you could have talked to Mr. Arneson, though."

"I'll catch up with him yet," Russ said.

They were moving single file down the narrow, stony trail, Russ in the lead. It was slow going because of the soggy treacherous footing. It would be worse still when darkness came, a little while from now. A horse saw in darkness as a man could not, but a horse could fall just the same, and a broken leg in a place like this—Penny shuddered to think of it.

"Watch it here," Russ called back to her.

She saw dimly what had stopped him: a washout in the trail where the rain had cut a small gully down the mountainside.

"That's the way canyons are formed!"—an echo of her father's voice from some long ago ride after rain.

Abruptly, it seemed, the thick gray dusk had turned to black night. Russ was keeping close, she knew, though she could scarcely see even his outline. A new uneasiness was shivering through Penny now, a sense of being followed. From the way Midnight was snorting and blowing, he sensed it, too. Suddenly Penny was sure. A rider or a riderless horse was coming after them, for she had heard a faint click of

hoof on rock. Russ had reined in. He spoke to her quietly:
"Want to take the lead, Penny?"

She did want to. It would be good to have Russ between
her and whatever it was back there. He must have seen, too,
how hard it was to hold Midnight in. A moment later he
called, "Let him set the pace, Penny. Within limits!" he
added, as Midnight plunged and tried to take his head.

It was now that it came, a wild screaming neigh out of the
dark behind them, a blood-chilling, exaggerated sound such
as no horse should ever make.

Midnight gave a shrill whinny and reared, Penny barely
held him from bolting headlong. She worked with him, bend-
ing forward, speaking into his ear, until she had control again.

"Good girl," Russ called.

Penny was damp to the skin and cold from the rain, but
the chill she felt now was the icy finger of terror itself. Even
so, with it there was a surge of something like triumph, for
what they had just heard was unquestionably the Screamer,
the creature that had been terrorizing the range, and Russ
had heard it, too! If they got safely down this mountain
there would be the word of two of them that the Phantom
Screamer was not her horse!

The sounds from behind were no longer stealthy. The
creature, stallion or demon, was close upon them and it was
impossible not to imagine him rearing above them with rip-
ping teeth and bludgeoning hoofs. They could go no faster.
The one thing that made these paralyzing moments endur-
able to Penny was that Russ was there, between her and the
thing, and that he had chosen to be.

In the next few moments Midnight had outdistanced Janus by some thirty yards. Despite her clamoring fear, the almost overpowering urge for flight that gripped her, Penny reined him in.

"You shouldn't have waited," Russ said, catching up. "I was hoping you'd just let him out—"

The sense of pursuit never flagged. From time to time eerie sounds reached them above the drip and rustle of the rain. The most frightening part of it was that not all of them were identifiable as horse sounds. Mixed with the unmistakable equine whooshings and snorts there was an intermittent moaning as of high wind through the pine tops, though there was no wind now. At any instant that scream might come again. Beneath her shock and terror, that neigh had touched a deeper chord in Penny. Though she could give it no name, it went on vibrating in her.

Once down off the steep trail they rode faster and abreast. The going was easier now, but the footing was still dangerous. Water had collected in the low spots and where the grass had died the horses sloshed through mud. But the scream had not been repeated and the sounds of pursuit were fainter now.

"The whole thing's fantastic," Russ said. "Are you all right, Penny?"

"Yes, but I never was so scared in my life!"

"You're not the only one who was scared!" Russ said. "We've got a mystery on our hands now for sure!"

"Do you think *it's* still coming after us?"

"Not pushing us anyhow. It's almost as if—" Russ broke off.

At least there had been enough rain to do some good. The ground was slushy and there were runneling sounds in the hollows. Also there were cattle sounds, good to Penny's ears, soft lowings of contentment to right and left.

"Have you got a theory, Russ?" she prompted him.

"Maybe. But it hasn't jelled enough to talk about."

In Penny's mind, too, there was something that hadn't jelled yet, but it was there. As they neared home Russ said, "The trouble is we've proved nothing except that Midnight is all Jekyll and no Hyde, and we knew that already!"

It was still raining when they took Midnight to the barn. Russ helped her unsaddle and feed him, but said: "I'm not coming in tonight, Penny. It's late and I'm all wet and muddy. Please make my excuses to your mother . . ."

Even before she got in the house Penny knew there was something wrong. Through the living room window she saw Ken pacing the floor and heard the sharp edge of his voice. Her mother's pale, worried face seemed to leap at her out of the shadows as she opened the door.

"Penny! I've been worried sick! Where is Russell?"

"He wants a rain check," Penny said. "He was soaked to the skin, and so am I."

Ken was too preoccupied to speak. His face in the lamplight looked gray with strain. Her mother came and took her by the shoulders. "I suppose it was the storm that delayed you," she said. "You *are* soaked to the skin!" Their eyes met levelly for an instant. "You are very pale, dear."

"That's because I was scared, Mother. I'll tell you all about it."

"Yes, later. Go upstairs now and change and I'll see about something hot for you to eat."

Aunt Celia came close for a moment, eyes questioning as her mother's had done. She said nothing but turned away apparently satisfied.

"Ken, what's *wrong?*" Penny asked.

"Later," her mother said. "He'll tell you later."

As she changed into dry clothes Penny tried to imagine what Ken was so furious about. It was anger more than anything else. She knew the signs, and somehow she felt that it concerned her, though how she could not see. She had done nothing to rouse his temper and Midnight had been accounted for for days.

Until Penny had eaten a bowl of hot noodle soup, a piece of kept-warm corn bread and some cold sliced ham, her mother wouldn't let her say a word.

"Eat your supper. Drink your milk," she kept saying. Then it was "Finish your dessert." Applesauce and caramel layer cake which Penny especially liked.

There was a fire in the grate tonight. Ken stood before it as Penny came into the living room, his arms ominously folded.

"We got chased," she said, not waiting any longer with her story. "We were coming down from Moon Creek. It was so dark we couldn't see it, but we heard it. I was never so scared in my life, and Russ admitted he was too. The horses acted perfectly crazy."

Laura Linstrom repeated rather vaguely, "Chased? How do you mean chased? By what?"

"IT, Mother. The Phantom Screamer! You couldn't call it a neigh. It's a horrible sound. There wasn't anything to do but run. Midnight almost bolted with me. What I mean is, everything they say about that beast must be true! And now we have the proof we need that it's *not* Midnight! Russ will swear to it, too."

Ken burst out, "I don't know what proof you've got, but it better be good! Jeff Stoddard and his foreman were over here this afternoon. It seems Link Joslin wasn't lying after all. Anyway, he's had them all steamed up about what he saw and heard last night and they're sure as ever that it was your horse. *My horse!* it is now! If you'd been home this afternoon instead of gallivanting over the mountain you might have done some good. I told Stoddard Midnight had been in for days and he said, 'Can you prove that? Let me see him right now!' So I had to tell him you were out riding. 'Stormin' like it is? Thunder and lightnin' and she out ridin' in it?' As good as called me a liar, the—the—"

"*Ken!*" Penny's mother said.

"But what happened last night, Ken?" Penny asked. "Did you find out from Mr. Stoddard?"

"What happened last night isn't the point, Penny! Nothing, probably! Nothing much anyhow! It's what happened today! Link Joslin up and quit! And another hand quit with him rather than do night herd duty! Scared silly, morale gone. The foreman himself has got to watch herd tonight! And that's not all! Jeff Stoddard left an ultimatum. From here on out all his hands are to carry rifles on range and be trigger-ready. 'If that crazy horse of yours is shot, Linstrom, you've had fair warning,' he told me. 'He'll be shot if he's seen on our land again, that's for sure! And Heskett goes along with me on that! I saw him and he says to tell you so!' *My* crazy horse!"

Penny was stunned to silence.

Her mother spoke: "What has happened, Penny, is the very thing that Ken dreaded most—real trouble with our neighbors! Nothing, nothing is worth that! Do you know Ken came within an inch of *hitting* Mr. Stoddard when he implied that he was lying? Can you imagine anything reaching such a point? It made me positively ill, and at the same time worrying about you! I haven't said much about it before, Penny, because I know how you feel about that horse, but I worry about you whenever you are out riding, and I cannot—I really cannot stand any more of it! He's such a nervous animal, so high strung! You said yourself a moment ago that he almost bolted with you! Well, this evening when you were so late in that storm and all, I said to Celia: 'If that child gets home alive and safe I shall see to it that she does not tempt Providence again! I shall forbid her riding that horse any more!'"

Penny could not believe her ears: "Mother! You don't know what you just said! You couldn't have meant that!"

"I do know what I said! I do, indeed! It is only because you are so wrapped up in that horse that I have not spoken long before! Now there is this second perfectly valid reason you should give him up—a near feud with our neighbors! We have to make some concession, Penny! You've got to let Midnight go . . ."

21

"Please Take My Horse"

THAT NIGHT PENNY CRIED FOR A LONG TIME INTO HER PILLOW. Give up Midnight! It was as unthinkable as giving up one of her own family, or Paintrock itself. Besides being her closest companion, he was a living connection with her father. Through Midnight's fleetness and willing power, the mountain world, her father's world, was always hers to enjoy and explore. Without this wonder, this consolation, how would she live through the days?

Worst of all, there was the new threat to Midnight's very life. "All hands armed and trigger-ready!" That meant that the Stoddards and the Hesketts, too, had made up their minds to shoot her horse on sight! And this had come in the very hour when she and Russ were proving that Midnight was "All Jekyll and no Hyde," as Russ had said. Mr. Hyde was out there all right, threatening and screaming, but how could they convince people? Until they knew the truth, Midnight was not safe outside his own corral. And how long would he stay there if she couldn't even exercise him?

Penny knew from experience how firm her mother could be, once she had made up her mind. Usually she was right, and that ended it. This time Mother did not understand and she was wrong. Like Ken, she was terribly upset over Mr. Stoddard's visit and the prospect of serious trouble with their neighbors. She had spoken hastily, wrongly. Yet to oppose her—and how could she not fight for Midnight—would mean real conflict.

In and through Penny's mind in this darkest of moments was the echo of that screaming neigh. It had touched some core of memory in her, but she could not bring it back. Too vague, too far away to be grasped. It might even have been a dream she had had long ago. She could only cry, and pray that Midnight would be kept safe.

When Penny awoke next morning the mountain told her it was six o'clock. The light was still dove color, but the upper rims were aflame with the climbing sun. As she went out to feed Midnight the rain-washed air was scented with sage and pine, and the ground underfoot was cushiony with moisture. Midnight's eager nicker sent a sharp pang through her.

"I will do everything I can to keep us together," she told him as he fed. "And you must do the same by not running away. Please, Midnight, please be patient! Be good!"

His gentle, liquid eye seemed receptive. Maybe horses understood what you said when it was important enough. Penny prayed that this was so. For the present, at least, she would not fight with her mother about riding him, or argue the issue with Ken. She would just wait and see what must be done.

At breakfast Ken and Solly talked about rounding up the steers for shipment. Because of drought conditions Ken had arranged for an early sale of beef stock. There was no mention of last night's upheaval. After breakfast Penny went back to the corral to groom her horse. There was a need in her to spend as much time with him as possible and try to reach him about the trouble they were in. At least he would feel her urgency.

At mid-morning Penny saw a station wagon coming up the lane. She didn't recognize the car and it was a shock of pleasure to see Russ getting out from behind the wheel. He looked all store-new in slacks and a sport shirt, walking toward the house.

Penny just couldn't let him see her like this, so she sneaked in the kitchen way and asked Mrs. Keeler to go to the door. Then she rushed up the back stairs to her own room to change. A few moments later her mother put her head in at the door.

"Russell is here, dear. He wonders if you'd care to drive to Brennerton with him this morning. I expect you'd like to go."

"Yes, mother, I'll be right down."

Drive to Brennerton with him! Penny was tingling with the surprise of it. She hustled into her blue linen suit and white pumps. High heels made her descent of the stairs quite sedate. Russ had made Mother feel much better about their being so late last night. As Penny came in he was telling how they had to take cover for awhile during the worst of the storm and how sorry he was for exposing her to the fright and danger of the ride down.

"I should have known better than to take her up that way."

"Well, Russell, I'm sure it was no fault of yours," Laura Linstrom said. "We missed having you come to supper with us. You must try to come again soon."

It was the first time they had ever been out in a car together and Penny was thrilled, but Russ seemed to be taking it all for granted. His mind was buzzing, she could tell, but it was not until they were out on the State Road that he began to talk.

"Well, there's a lot more to this business than we knew last night! That hunch, remember? Instead of going right home after I left you I took the old horse-trail into the cottonwoods for a way and waited there. I had a feeling that whoever or whatever had been following us would keep on coming, but at a slower pace, and would most likely keep to the trees east of your place. Well, in about ten minutes I heard horse sounds, just ordinary ones, but coming closer.

I dismounted and stood at Janus' head to keep him quiet, and Penny, *I saw him!* He was some thirty feet away among the trees but I got a pretty clear impression of him. Our demon horse *is* black and that's not all! He has a rider!"

For a moment Penny let a flood of relief and thankfulness sweep over her. There *was* another black horse and Russ had seen him. Somehow Russ would find a way of proving that Midnight was blameless. But the black horse's *rider* . . .

Russ was going on: "I might have had a closer look, but the stallion sensed Janus and whinnied and the rider turned him quickly round and started back toward the hills. All the same, Penny, I know this much about him: He's long and skinny and wears a beard! It's that fellow Arneson, I'm convinced."

"Oh, Russ, it couldn't be! Why should Mr. Arneson follow us down the mountain and deliberately try to scare us. What *reason* could he have?"

"Only one answer to that, Penny. It's some kind of fear campaign. The man's out to scare people and cause as much trouble as he can."

"But *why*, Russ?"

"O.K. The motive. That's what we're going to try to find out. I've got a lead. Something Dad said this morning. Right now we're on our way to the *Brennerton News* office to do a bit of research on the Moon Creek Water Project . . ."

At the newspaper office Russ asked for permission to go over the files of some five years back. They were shown into a basement storage room and left to do their own searching among the dated stacks. At one end of the room was a long high table with a light above and here they laid out the cumbersome sheets to scan the editorials of five years ago.

"Looks hopeless without an exact date," Russ said. "But Dad says it was front page news for a while, so we'll come up with it."

Even so, it was an hour or more before they came upon the information they wanted. It seemed that the Ranchers' Association had formed a company to divert Moon Creek water for the benefit of the larger rangeland holdings below the Wapitis. On the list of ranchers involved they found both their fathers' names. And Jeff Stoddard and James Heskett were the nominal heads of the company.

The action taken had not been illegal, for the Ranchers' Association had offered to buy out the back hills settlers most affected. The majority of the homesteaders had sold to them. A few, however, including Dolf Arneson, had fought the project and held out.

"So we've established a motive," Russ said. He had several pages of annotations carefully dated. "We've got something to go on now."

It was past lunch time and they stopped at Ketterman's for a milk shake and a hamburger. Under any other circumstances, having lunch with Russ at one of Ketterman's small tables would have been a real event to Penny, but before her now were Dolf Arneson's eyes. They were sad, as if he had seen all the troubles of Job. His accusing words were understandable now: "Rob a man of his water and you take his life's blood. Your father turned against his friend." It had been a shock to Penny to see the name of Carl Linstrom on that list. After all, Paintrock always had water, not as much as it could use, but enough to get by. To Dolf Arneson and those others, the diversion of Moon Creek had meant ruin.

"I wish something could be done about it!" Penny said.

Russ misunderstood. "Never fear, Penny, we're going to do something about it! Dolf Arneson was one of the chief losers in that water deal, which no doubt accounts for the bitterness he showed when you went up there. Push it a little further and you've got a vengeance campaign. Heskett and Stoddard, remember, were the prime movers in the deal. Your dad and mine just went along with the rest."

"I wish they hadn't!" Penny said.

"Maybe they were obliged to, Penny. In a case like that the majority rules. It was a logical step for the R. A. to take. There were very few who lost by it compared to the men who have benefited, and the nesters had their chance to sell. What we need to know now is the how and wherefore of that other black horse. Then the Sheriff can take over."

"Arrest Mr. Arneson?"

"Naturally, Penny. Why, what's the matter?"

Something had just occurred to Penny that would draw all the strands together in the very way Russ was working for. But much as she wanted to help him, Penny knew that she could have no part in Mr. Arneson's arrest. He had been through too much already; he had lost all. Not even for Midnight could Penny agree in her heart to bring this final misery and disgrace upon her father's old friend.

"Russ," Penny said. "You've always thought that Shiloh is Midnight's sire. That's sort of like having a share in him, isn't it? Russ, I want you to take Midnight—take him as a gift!"

Russ looked at her incredulously.

"*Why*, Penny, *why?*"

"Because it's the only way I know to save Midnight's life! Yesterday while we were up at Arneson's place Mr. Stoddard and his foreman came over and warned Ken that they're going to shoot Midnight on sight if he's seen on their land again, and the Hesketts will do the same. You know at our place there's no sure way to keep Midnight in. He'll get loose again and be shot! But your stockades are safe and sure. Take him, Russ, please take him!"

Russ' look at her was full of sympathy and understanding. "I remember you said Arneson was a friend of your father's and I know what you're doing, you're trying to protect the man! But look, Penny! Whether it's Arneson or not, whoever is causing all this trouble must be apprehended soon. It's our duty to stop him before something really tragic happens. It's not only the injustice to Midnight; any time somebody may get killed. For the man's sake as well as our own we've got to report what we know to the authorities."

Penny was fighting back the tears. "I can't do it, Russ. I can't! Will you take Midnight, please?"

"Sure, Penny," Russ said, "if that's the way you really want it."

22

Heart Stretch

WHEN PENNY TOLD HER MOTHER SHE HAD GIVEN MIDNIGHT TO Russ Armstrong, Laura Linstrom said nothing, simply held her close for a moment in her fondest way. Afterwards she said, "Your aunt and Ken are in the other room. Let's see what they think about it."

"Well, that's one way out," Ken said. "Little old long-hearted Penny! She may not *think* things through to a conclusion, but when it comes to *feeling* she's right every time."

Aunt Celia said, "Don't you fool yourself, Ken. Penny's head is in the right place, too!"

Late that afternoon Russ came over for Midnight.

"Of course you're to ride him whenever you feel like it, Penny," he said.

Penny had anticipated this and she had her answer ready. "It seems to me it would be better if I don't ride him or even see him," she said. "Whoever feeds and grooms him should be the first to ride him. He'll want to be ridden, though, Russ, so he won't fight it. Pretty soon he'll be *asking* for his bridle."

Russ was in the saddle with Midnight's hackamore strap in his hand. "Don't decide about it right now," he said.

"I have to, Russ. I have decided!"

"O.K., Penny," Russ said. "See you soon."

As Midnight was led away a cord attached to her very heart seemed stretching, stretching. Penny stood waiting for it to break. For Midnight's own sake the cut should be clean. He must learn to accept a new life, a new rider. Not seeing her at all, he would make the adjustment sooner. So let her heart break if it must. But somehow the cord did not break, it just went on pulling.

For something to do she raked up the corral and put things in order in the shelter. By suppertime Penny had fought it out with herself to a point beyond tears and could face the family again.

The rounding up of steers for the September beef shipment was to begin in the morning. Ken was short-handed, she knew. Maybe he would let her help in the roundup. This would be a small operation, the real roundup came in the spring, but there would be lots to learn and she needed the chance to forget herself.

"Just what I need, an extra hand," Ken said when she asked. "Sis, you're hired."

"Driving in steers," Laura Linstrom said. "What a horrible idea!"

"Why, Mother? It has to be done. I'm sure I can get the hang of it soon, and Ken says he can use me."

"Why, she'll make a fine cow-waddy!" Ken said. "You can ride Stonewall, Penny, and start out with me in the morning."

Her mother's head was in her hands. "Cow-waddy!"

"Now, Laura," Aunt Celia said firmly. "'Miss Wyoming!' I believe you called her! And I was to remember that both your children were born to ranch life! At the time I thought your attitude was praiseworthy. But it does seem to me you've been slipping a bit, lately."

"I'm afraid so, Celia. Well, I suppose it will be all right so long as Ken rides with her . . ."

Next morning Penny and Ken were in the saddle before the sun had topped the Elkhorn rims. Both wore heavy leather chaps today for there would be much thorny brush to ride through, and bandannas to pull over the mouth and nose when the herd kicked up a fog of dust. Every item of cowboy gear had its practical reason for being. The ten-gallon hats they wore would be sunshades or umbrellas as needed, and in a pinch would hold drinking water. The high heels of their boots slanted forward so that their weight in the saddle rested on the ball of the foot, less tiring that way than on the instep. Neither wore spurs, a peculiarity of Paintrock Ranch, but Ken had a lasso looped beside his saddle horn.

The peaks flamed golden as they rode up-country. Already the horses sensed what was on and seemed eager and willing. Ken, however, had his early morning glum on and Penny's heart was low. Who would be giving Midnight his breakfast this morning? He would be watching for her, but there would be exciting new horse-sounds to keep him interested.

Up at the edge of the grassland Vic, Charlie and Bud had already collected a little bunch of mixed cattle, the nucleus of the first "gather." Even these few animals were keeping the three busy.

"Wild bunch," Vic said to Ken. "Found these up on a narrow ledge where not even a goat ought to be. Had to hang on by our lass ropes to chivvy 'em off it."

Penny and Ken rode higher into rough brush country. She wished her brother would talk as they went like her father used to, but Ken was entirely occupied with the business of spotting hiding steers.

"In here," he said at last. "You take the left side. I'll keep to the right."

It was a brush-grown ravine. Penny herself had seen nothing, but with scarcely a sign from her Stonewall picked his way across a dry stream-bed and along a rocky slope into dense thickets. Still no sign of anything so far as Penny was aware, until three steers broke cover so abruptly that it startled her. These plunged up-slope and would soon have

lost themselves again except that Ken appeared from the
thickets above. He whooped and the steers turned in their
sudden way, intent on getting around him. Stonewall, however, with a burst of speed, cut the three off, and Penny and
Ken tailed them down grade.

"You'll do!" Ken said.

"I didn't do a thing! Stonewall did it! How'd you know
the steers were in there? Did you see them?"

"No, just felt 'em. Smoky knew they were in there. Half
the time he knows before I do."

Penny remembered her father saying that a real circle-
rider feels cattle before he sees them, something like a hunt-
er's sixth sense. It surprised her to see this faculty in Ken.
Though these steers were almost deerlike in their agile
speed from months of freedom, Ken seemed to anticipate
their every dodge and break and was always there to cut
them off.

By now the gather had become a sizable bunch, for Solly
and Rudy had also been at work in the rounding up.

"There's more where these come from," Solly said. "Five
or six got away from us."

"Up Box Canyon way, I'll bet," Ken said.

"Nowheres else. And do those babies know how to hide!"

"Must have been tipped off by ground telegraph."

"This bunch has got antelope blood in 'em," Charlie File
said.

Penny and Ken were off again along the trail that led to
Cedar Glen, but they didn't reach the glen this trip. "I see
a white face in that buck brush," Penny called.

"O.K.," Ken said. "Take right this time."

They converged upon the spot and a cow and her leggy calf broke cover. This was a calf dropped after the spring roundup, grown wild through the summer months. The pair made for cover higher up. Penny, who was closest, maneuvered to cut them off, but with a surprising burst of speed the cow outstripped Stonewall and was lost to sight again. This was stony, steep terrain, hard on the horses. For the next hour they threaded through brush and boulders until Penny was sorry she had ever glimpsed that white face, and said so.

"All in the day's work," Ken said. He worked with a doggedness and patience that amazed her. This was a side of Ken that Penny had never seen before and it made her feel proud of her brother.

At last Ken was able to use his rope. After the calf had been dragged into the open, it was a matter of waiting for his bawling to bring the mother in.

"There are always plenty of these," Ken said. "We wouldn't bother with them, only the calf's past due for branding."

Their next try was luckier, four steers and a couple of dry cows bunched under some hemlocks. After cutting out the cows to run free, they worked the steers back to the gather, by this time a bawling, shuffling confusion of dust and noise.

Penny was tired, but fascinated, and learning fast, as much from Stonewall as from Ken, with a new respect for both. In fact everything Ken had ever said about "his kind of horse" was proving true. The cow pony *was* great.

The work took skilled riding, hard riding, every minute.

No time to think about Midnight watching and waiting for her, wondering why she had deserted him, or of the lonesome saddle on its improvised rack in the shelter, or of the empty days ahead for them both. Time only for short sharp flashes out of the corner of her mind.

"Get through the first three days." That was what her father used to say when something bad happened, like the time he lost over half of the herd in a blizzard and cash money was too low to restock. "You can go on standing most anything after three days, if it hasn't killed you by that time," he used to say.

23

The World Is Whole and Bright

THOSE THREE DAYS PASSED IN A DAZE OF EXERTION; IN THE saddle from first light to sunset, thinking and talking of little but cattle, going to her room at the earliest chance to sleep in grateful exhaustion. Midnight is safe, she would think the last thing before sleep, the first thing in the morning. At least, he is safe.

Now, at the end of a week, Paintrock's fenced pasture-land, which included a portion of the creek-bed down by the seep, was full of restless bawling steers to be fattened for shipment. These were the best beef cattle; the scrubs had been cut out and turned back to range.

Today they had gotten around to the calves in the branding corral. Outside the corral the mothers waited, already anxious and bawling. Vic tended the wood fire in which the branding irons were turning ash-gray and cherry-red. At Paintrock they did not hold with deep branding or with the newer commercial branding fluids. "A light stamp with a gray-hot iron, just a good scorch," Carl Linstrom used to say. "The only one that really feels any pain is the calf's mother, bawlin' outside the corral." It was the anxious mothers that Penny's heart went out to at this time, but their short torment was more than made up for by the joy of reunion with their calves.

It was Solly who "heeled" the calf, roping it by its hind legs. The "flankers" this season were Bud and Charlie File. They threw and held the calf while Vic applied the stamping iron briefly to its left side. Paintrock did not earmark its calves, and the brand was the same as devised by Grandpa Linstrom years ago, "A P and an R, back to back."

The circle-riding was over now, and though tired to the bone, Penny was sorry. For now she must face her loss the more keenly, living down each hour without the diversion of constant riding. She was watching the cows nuzzling and soothing their returned calves and licking them endlessly from head to foot. Penny was lost in the sight, so that Solly had to call twice to get her attention.

"Miss Penny, the Armstrong station wagon just drove in with young Russ at the wheel. That's bound to mean you, ain't it?"

Penny got down from the corral bars and stood for a moment with thumping heart. It was too early in the day for a purely social call from Russ. Something must have happened. Maybe Midnight had broken away or injured himself. Or maybe they had found they just couldn't keep him, stockades or not. She was running, but the gay tootle of Russ' horn and the sight of his smiling face reassured her. She slowed down and tried to collect herself, realizing how she must look—like the ranch-hand I am, she thought. Russ grinned at her.

"You look as if you'd been pretty busy. Midnight's O. K.," he answered the unspoken question in her eyes. "This is something else. Will you drive in to Brennerton with me?"

"I'd like to, Russ," Penny said. "I'll tell mother and get ready. Are you coming in?"

"I'll wait here," he said. "I'll explain everything as we go."

"Well, these town trips are getting to be a regular thing!" Laura Linstrom said. "Isn't Russell coming in?"

"He said he'd wait in the car. May I remind him about his rain check, Mother?"

"Of course, dear. Tell Russell he's welcome any time."

Penny changed quickly into a white frock that contrasted with her summer tan. She was churning with speculation.

Whatever Russ had in mind, it must concern Dolf Arneson, and on that matter she could be no more cooperative than before. After much thought, the stand she had taken still seemed right to her; she would neither say nor do anything to add to Mr. Arneson's afflictions.

Rejoining Russ, Penny felt tense, for she hated to disappoint him again and was sure that she must.

"Mother says your rain check's good any time," she said, adding, "when I saw you coming I thought Midnight had gotten away in spite of everything!"

"No, Midnight's fine," Russ said. "I've been feeding and grooming him myself and we're just like *that!* But I want to be sure he won't fight me before I try riding him."

"I'm glad you could be the one to take care of him these first days," Penny said. "I'll bet it's taken up a lot of your time though."

"Gee, no. What took time was following up those leads we got from the newspaper files."

"What—happened?" Penny asked.

Russ must have heard the apprehension in her tone, for his glance was very understanding. "I did what had to be done, Penny. I gave the sheriff the facts of the situation, along with an account of recent events on the range and our being chased down-trail that night and later catching sight of a tall thin man on a black horse. Just a straight account with the R. A. Ditch as a possible motive for revenge."

"Did they—arrest him?"

"Well, it took several days for the sheriff's men to come

up with him. All they really wanted was to ask him some questions, but he began to talk wildly and kick up a fuss, so they took him in. Since then, he's clammed up. The sheriff is sure he knows something, so he's holding him as a suspect. In the meantime, the 'Phantom Screamer' is as much a mystery as ever.

"I tried talking to him, myself. I told him I knew it was he who had followed us down the Moon Creek trail. All he did was stare at me, then turn his face to the wall. Arneson's a very bitter man, Penny, and I've no doubt he feels justified in making trouble for the ranchers. But he's doing himself a great disservice keeping quiet about it all. If he won't talk, the authorities have no choice but to hold him. They've got to find out about that horse—before someone else gets hurt. And that, Penny, is where you come in."

"No, Russ, I don't come into this at all," Penny said. "On your account I wish I could, but I feel just the same as before about Mr. Arneson. I won't do anything or say anything to make more trouble for him."

"But, Penny, you'll be helping him! As far as I know you're the only person who can help Arneson. If we convince him that you're his friend—and you've certainly proved that—he may talk. And if he tells you his story, makes a clean breast of the whole thing, it will go a lot easier for him, you can be sure of that. So, if you're willing, we're going to visit Dolf Arneson at the Brennerton jail."

Put this way, that it was up to her to help Mr. Arneson, there seemed nothing to do but try, though the thought of seeing him in jail and those sad eyes accusing her once more, was almost unbearable. She had not spoken and Russ asked: "So will you go with me, Penny?"

"I won't have to accuse him of anything, will I?"

"Of course not. You'll be there as his friend."

At the Brennerton jail Penny was addressed respectfully as Miss Linstrom and thanked for her cooperation in coming. She and Russ waited for a while in the Sheriff's office. At last Dolf Arneson was brought in. He did not respond to their greeting. Penny was spared the accusation of the suffering eyes for he would not even look at her.

Russ said: "We're here to try and help you, Mr. Arneson. Miss Linstrom is a real friend of yours and I'm going to prove it to you. But we can't help unless you tell us your side of the story."

"I'm not asking for your help."

"I understand now what you meant about being robbed of water, Mr. Arneson," Penny said. "I didn't know what you meant the day I was up at your place. I'd never heard about the Moon Creek Project then." She was close to tears and had to swallow several times before she could go on. "But I am your friend, Mr. Arneson, and my father was your friend no matter how it seems to you. He would never have robbed you of anything. I know that."

Still no response from Dolf Arneson.

"I said I could prove Penny Linstrom is your friend," Russ was saying now. "You probably know that her black horse, Midnight, has been blamed for all the range mishaps and two of the neighboring ranchers threatened to shoot him on sight. But rather than point a finger at you, Penny gave up

her horse—a very great sacrifice, I can assure you."

Dolf Arneson's eyes came round at last, settling on Penny's face. "That was the horse you rode up to my place?"

"Yes," Penny said.

"And how," he asked shrewdly, eyes still holding her face, "did you think to help me by giving up your horse?"

"Because I knew about Pitchdark," Penny said. "But how did you *do* it, Mr. Arneson? How did you tame him? A wild stallion that no one was ever able to get near? How did you *do* it?"

A faint smile came over Arneson's face and it lit up his eyes in a way that Penny remembered. "It took time, much time. But that I have had, and not much else, since my wife die and my Minna go away. A man has to have something. Once I tell your father 'there is no such thing as a wild horse if he has one human friend.' Pitchdark have me. Even in those days that horse come down and drink my water, eat my salt. Three years work it was to get a saddle on him. And then he like to kill me! But I sat him twice and he was mine. Not in any corral, mind you. Free like now, but mine. Come to my call. I even shod him. I want to get back at those men who rob and ruin me and I think of a way." His eye narrowed again. "You know about Pitchdark, but *how* you know?"

"That's what I want to know!" Russ said.

"It was the scream," Penny said. "When I heard it on the Moon Creek trail I started to remember. Once years ago, Mr. Arneson, you made that call for my father. You said it was a way you had to call the wild horses in." She turned to Russ. "It wasn't until we were having lunch in Ketterman's that time and you were talking that I really remembered and it all came together. If Pitchdark is free in the hills, Mr. Arneson, will he go on making trouble for us all?"

"No," Arneson said. "Pitchdark did not make the trouble. He do only what I make him do. Maybe I do wrong. I have nothing against you. When you was little, you was like my Minna. Nothing false in you. I think that is still so."

It was three days later that Russ brought Midnight home. He had proposed bringing him the day of their visit to Brennerton, but Penny wanted to be sure that the truth was known to everyone before trusting Midnight in his old corral again. The matter of the other black horse was taken care of by the *Brennerton News*, which ran a front page story of Dolf Arneson's revelation and Penny Linstrom's part in it. The editor retracted his former story of "the Jekyll and Hyde Horse." Not only did he clear Midnight of all blame but he was kind and understanding in his handling of Dolf Arneson, creating a sympathetic picture of a lonely man harrassed beyond endurance. Arneson, who had been released from jail, deserved a helping hand from his fellow ranchers, the paper said.

The news story started a series of neighborly calls at Paintrock and there were many halting but heartfelt apologies. The Stoddards and the Hesketts were particularly contrite about the hasty and unreasonable threat they had made, and asked Penny not to hold it against them.

Much to Penny's surprise, her mother, too, was sorry about having insisted that she give up her horse.

"I was worried to distraction that night, dear, and spoke much too harshly. But you were wonderful about it. I can't tell you how relieved I am that you're to have Midnight back, to ride and care for the same as ever, and I want to say how very proud of you I am."

Now Penny was out by Midnight's corral, dressed and ready, for a ride was planned and afterward Russ would have supper with them. When she saw him coming over the rise to the south, leading Midnight, the rush of joy that filled Penny made the world whole and bright again. No wonder that heart-cord had stretched and stretched without breaking when Midnight was led away. It was because he was soon to come back to her. You could not lose what really belonged to you, not even in death, because wasn't her father still the heart and soul of Paintrock Ranch?

Midnight had seen her now. She heard his glad whinny of greeting.

HALL-HALSELL SCHOOL